CL16

Brockworth Library, Moorfield Road,
Brockworth, Gloucester. GL3 4EX
Tel: 01452 863681 Email:
office@brockworthlink.org.uk
www.brockworthlink.org.uk

Brockworth
link

LARGE PRINT

Items should be returned to any Gloucestershire County Library on or
before the date stamped below. This book remains the property of the
Brockworth Community Library and can be renewed in person or by
telephone by calling **01452 862 730**

CRIME

LIP

THE LIFE BUYER

Ruthless entrepreneur Marcus King was obsessed with staying alive and used his millions to buy life from the bodies of others. When a highly scientific plan to kill him fails, police chief Dale Markham tries to discover who is behind the assassination attempt. But with the case's far-reaching implications, special agent Steve Delmonte is assigned to work with the police. There follows a trail of murders all the way to the moon before the incredible truth can be revealed.

E. C. TUBB

THE LIFE BUYER

Complete and Unabridged

LINFORD
Leicester

First published in Great Britain

Tubb, E.C.
  The life buyer.—Large print ed.—
  Linford mystery library
  1. Detective and mystery stories
  2. Large type books
  I. Title
  823.9'14 [F]

  ISBN 1–84617–488–0

Published by
F. A. Thorpe (Publishing)
Anstey, Leicestershire

Set by Words & Graphics Ltd.
Anstey, Leicestershire
Printed and bound in Great Britain by
T. J. International Ltd., Padstow, Cornwall

This book is printed on acid-free paper

1

Marcus Edward King, eighty-seven years old, rich as Croesus, devoid of faith, sat up in bed and screamed into the darkness.

'No!'

Glass crashed as he fumbled at a bedside table, water gurgling, phials rattling, a book thudding softly to the floor. A button sank beneath a searching finger and soft rose-light flooded the room.

'No!'

The light brightened, comforting him with the revelation of familiar things; the statuette carved from Luna stone, the exotic insect trapped in a block of water-clear plastic, which stared at him with blind, iridescent eyes, wings a shimmering skein of colour. A solar clock rested diamond glitters on the hour of four.

'No,' he said for the third time. 'Damn it, no!'

He sat crouched on the bed, knees

drawn up to his chin, arms wrapped around his knees, the covers a crumpled mess at his feet. Warm air circulated through the chamber and dried the sweat on his body.

'Sir?'

A shadow loomed before an open door, anxious eyes searching the room, the ebon face and sombre clothing a vague silhouette against the background dimness of the antechamber.

'I'm all right.' Marcus glanced at the solar clock. The guard had been fast — but he was paid to be fast. Here, at the summit of the Palace, assassination was a remote possibility but there were other dangers and seconds could spell the difference between life and . . .

'I'm all right,' he repeated irritably then softened his tone. One day, perhaps, his life could depend on this man. 'You were fast,' he soothed. 'I shall remember that.'

'Thank you, sir.'

'That will be all,' said Marcus. 'You may go.'

The guard hesitated.

'I said — never mind.' Marcus

restrained his impatience. It was pointless to pay a man to do a job and then prevent him from doing it. And the man was right to be cautious. Fuming he waited as the guard searched the room; a human bloodhound smelling for traps and dangers.

'I had a dream,' said Marcus when he had finished. 'A nightmare, nothing more.'

'Yes, sir.'

'It woke me up.'

'Yes, sir. I heard. Could I get you anything?'

'No — yes. Get me Fullen.'

'Right away, Mr. King.'

Marcus nodded dismissal, rising as the door closed, bare feet silent as he padded towards the shower. Chemicals laved him, water caressed him, scented air dried with sterile heat. A wall-mirror reflected his image for critical inspection.

He bared his teeth at what he saw.

The teeth were natural growths; fresh buds transplanted into his gums from the jaws of a child at a basic cost of five thousand to the mother. The hair was growing from the scalp of a twenty-year-old man who had sold it for three thousand and a dozen wigs. The heart had cost much more; bought from a worker cursed with cancerous lungs, a sense of responsibility and a beautiful young wife. The stomach had been relatively cheap, the kidneys had come from a voluntary donor, the varicosed veins which had once mottled his legs had been replaced by plastic surrogates.

For its age it was a good body. It had cost him over a quarter of a million.

* * *

Fullen was waiting when he left the shower. The medic was tall, smoothly made and his voice had the compulsion of an organ. Deep-set eyes invited trust and promised understanding. He was the topmost psychiatrist of his time before Marcus had offered him double his salary to renounce general practice — three times the salary of the President of the Federated Earth Republics.

'You sent for me, Mr. King?'

4

'Yes.' Marcus settled himself on the couch. 'I had a nightmare. I screamed . . . '

'Screaming and inevitably in shock.' Fullen seated himself at the head of the couch. 'Well, we must find the cause of the dream and eliminate it if we can. Shock is something we must avoid. Relax now and let yourself drift. Breath evenly, don't strain, just settle yourself as if for sleep. That's it. That's fine. Now relax a little more . . . a little more . . . That's better. You feel as if you are floating. Nothing can bother you. Nothing matters. You are utterly detached. Good. Now tell me about your dream. Tell me what you saw and felt and heard. Tell me . . . '

And suddenly, it was all there. All the ghastly horror of it. The sickening loneliness. The helpless despair as, within him, a countless host of tiny suns winked into darkness; expiring with the universe of his being. Then came the burrowing maggots, the thriving bacteria, the rot and putrescence of decay. The cloying stench of lilies, the numbing echo of sonorous bells, the casket, the soft, wet obscene delving of spades.

And after —

'No!'

'Steady!' Fuller was there, warm, human, alive. 'It's all right, Mr. King. It's all right"

The guard looked into the room, saw that his master was all right, silently withdrew. Neither man noticed the intrusion.

'That was bad,' said Marcus. 'Bad.'

'But not as bad as the original waking,' said Fullen quickly. His hands made firm, comforting pressures on the figure on the couch. 'Pulse high, respiration ragged, but that was to be expected. You achieved almost total recall.'

'Is that good?'

'Very good, Mr. King. By reliving the incident you have diminished its importance. In fact — '

'Rubbish!'

Fullen was patient.

'Gunk!' snapped Marcus. 'I could have told you what I dreamed without all this rigmarole.'

'You are in a temper,' said Fullen evenly. 'You are angry, not at me, but at yourself. I am merely a convenient scapegoat.'

'So?'

'Every psychiatrist is a whipping boy. Your reaction is not unique.'

'All right,' snarled Marcus. 'So I'm angry at myself. Can you tell me why?'

'Yes. You are afraid of death.'

'Brilliant!' Marcus swung himself upright on the couch. 'Do I really pay you a fortune to tell me that?'

'You do not like to be afraid,' continued Fullen calmly. 'You are angry with yourself for yielding to that emotion. My statement as to the cause of that fear is correct. You are afraid of death.'

'I hate it — not fear it.'

'We always hate the thing we fear, Mr. King.'

'And kill the thing we love?'

'Not always. Would you — '

'Forget it!' Marcus jerked to his feet and began to pace the floor. 'Tell me about the dream.'

'It was a fear-symbol. The betrayal of a personality which is suffering from a morbid fear of death.'

'Morbid?' Marcus halted his pacing. 'Is it unhealthy to fear death? Is it unnatural to want to live? Damn it, Fullen, carry what you say to its logical conclusion and every healthy person wants to die!'

'Quite a number of them do, the death-wish is very strong, but normal people have the patience to wait. They neither seek death nor worry themselves into insanity trying to avoid it. Those that do usually have a reason based on beliefs which you do not appear to hold.' Fullen paused. 'They fear to die,' he said deliberately, 'because they are afraid of what waits for them on the other side.'

'Nothing is on the other side.'

'No, Mr. King.'

'Nothing,' snapped Marcus. 'Nothing at all.'

Irritably he resumed his pacing, passing the sightless monster, the statuette carved in the shape of a girl by some woman-hungry astronaut. His bare feet thudded on the carpet, anger weighing his tread.

'You said 'appear',' he accused. 'You doubt it?'

'I am not sure. There is something buried deep down inside your mind which I cannot reach. You won't permit me to reach it. But why should you dream of a grave?'

'People are buried in graves.'

'Not for the past fifty years. Cremation has been obligatory that long. But you dreamt of a grave. And lilies, another odd factor, odder still when coupled with the casket and the bells. You fear death but couple that fear with a burial in the past, not the future.' Fullen looked thoughtful, his eyes detached. 'An interesting juxta-position of diverse time-sectors which I feel would be profitable to investigate.'

'No.'

'But — '

'Forget it!'

'I really think that you should permit me to — '

'Fullen,' snarled Marcus savagely, 'you are a fool! I didn't hire you to read my mind or to amuse yourself with your probing. You had some interesting theories on psychosomatic ageing which I wanted you to investigate — or have you forgotten?'

'I have not forgotten, Mr. King.'

'When can I expect results?'

'Personal results?' Fullen hesitated. 'I never claimed I could arrive at a quick solution of the problem. I suspect that ageing is caused by the conditioning that commences at birth, and which teaches that age is always accompanied by physical degeneration. But not everyone grows senile; not everyone exhibits the same degree of degeneration. There is a variable which I suspect could be attributed to an attitude of mind.'

'You have nothing concrete for me?'

'No, Mr. King. Not at the moment.'

* * *

Alone Marcus scowled at the solid wall of crystal running the entire length of the room. He barked a word; the sonic device altered the polarization, the wall becoming transparent to the world outside.

Below lay the city, still dark, still twinkling with the fireflies of advertising displays, streetlights, windows, moving vehicles. The drifting lights of aircraft were a shimmering cloud of luminescent smoke. Higher the dawn was breaking, just visible from where he stood, a wash of pink and gold rising from the east. There were no clouds. It promised to be a fine day.

A bird, fooled by the transparency, dashed itself against the glass and fell with lifeless wings. Marcus hardly noticed. He was thinking of the dream and of others he had had before. They were all much the same. Dying and death and what waited beyond.

Closing his eyes he leaned against the smooth coolness of the crystal and let his mind skip back through time. Achieve total recall, Fullen had said. Discharge the emotional impact of an incident and diminish its importance. Relive it and forget it. Simple.

But could you forget murdering your father?

He smelt again the sickly scent associated with hospitals, felt the irritation of waiting, the shock of seeing what the doctors had done. They had been proud of their achievement.

'The finest piece of medical engineering to date,' one had said. He smiled at the machine beside the bed, the tubes running into the chest cavity, the grey face with sunken eyes on the pillow. He had turned and bumped into Marcus, quick with an apology because the King name, even then, had spelt power. And old J.K. owned the hospital.

Old J.K. Joseph King, seventy-five years old, finally living up to his reputation. Now, literally, he had no heart. Instead he had a machine that pumped oxygenated blood through body and brain.

Marcus hated that machine.

'How long?'

The doctor misunderstood — he tried to be optimistic.

'No one can be sure but, if there are no complications, well, your guess is as good as mine. But theoretically there is no limit. Five years. Ten. Fifty even. It is possible.'

A day was twenty-four hours too long.

Alone he had looked at the man in the

12

bed, the machine at his side. It was powered by electricity and to cut the juice would be to advertise murder. But the tubes were plastic and, if they were nipped — so, and held — so, who could prove it was other than accident?

Marcus did what had to be done.

He waited until the grey face on the pillow had become lax with a hollow emptiness before calling the doctors. He had been distraught. They had been very understanding, very sympathetic. They had reason to be.

The King was dead — long live the King!

Long live Marcus Edward King, now the undisputed head of the King financial empire.

And, of course, the new owner of the hospital in which they worked.

That had been sixty-four years ago.

*   *   *

Marcus opened his eyes and stared at the brightening day. Memory had taken time and, outside, the world was coming to life. A supply plane approached the Palace, the crown insignia gaudy in the sunshine, slowing with a tilt of vanes as it angled towards the landing stage. A cargo train crossed the sky in the distance. A police helijet drifted lazily to one side, waspish in black and yellow.

It was a busy, normal scene.

He looked at it, sensing the throb and pulse of life, the intermeshed activity. It was a world in which money was power and he had money.

Money to buy anything and everything he wanted.

Everything!

Impatiently he turned from the window, strode towards a communicator, pressed a button. A startled face stared at him from the screen — the operator had not been expecting a summons but he was eager to please.

'Yes, sir, Mr. King?'

'Get me — '

Marcus paused, eyes narrowed as he looked through the wall of crystal. Some forgotten instinct directed his attention to a point high to the east, where, almost invisible against the sun, a tiny black fleck marred the blue of the sky.

'Yes, sir. Mr. King?'

The operator was patient. Marcus ignored him. He was staring at the black fleck, wondering if it were another bird intent on smashing itself to a pulp of blood and feather. Almost immediately he knew it could not be that. Already it was too big, growing too fast, the flight too steadily aimed at the window.

And birds did not have rigid wings or trail streamers of flame.

He turned and ran from the communicator, his fear too great for the strength of his body. He collided with the bed, tripped, sprawled on the floor. He rose and fell again, the discarded sheet hampering his feet. An alarm sounded and he turned, eyes bulging as he stared at the plane, now monstrous beyond the window.

'No!' he screamed. 'Dear God! No!'

He caught a flash of black and yellow as the police helijet darted forward. It dissolved in a gush of flame and sound and fury blasted him against the far wall.

'Sir!'

The guard was at his side, ebon face strained as he lifted Marcus from the debris, cradling him as if he were a child.

'Are you all right, sir?'

'Out!' screamed Marcus. 'Quick, you fool!'

Dazed and shaken he could still anticipate the terror to come. The air reeked with the stench of fuel.

'Out! Damn you! Out!'

The guard obeyed. He lunged toward the antechamber, feet slipping on the littered floor, shielding Marcus with his own body.

The flame and heat and whining metal completed the destruction of the room.

2

The place was a mess. Plaster littered the broken floor and naked girders rested in splintered concrete. The air stank with the scent of burning and the foam used to kill the flames hung like dirty candy-floss from the walls; an icing to the cake of destruction. A group of technicians clustered around the wreckage of the plane at the far end of the room. A chill wind blew through the shattered window.

Steve Delmonte stood for a moment examining the scene then stepped carefully over a sheeted figure and walked to where Dale Markham stood among his staff. The chief of local police turned at the crunch of broken glass, smiled a greeting.

'Steve!' They shook hands with genuine warmth. 'It's good to see you again. Is this visit official or were you just passing by?'

'Official.'

'I thought so.' Markham looked curiously at the special agent of the Federated Republics. 'What's Security interested in this for?'

'Security is interested in everything,' said Steve blandly. 'Especially when a thing like this happens to a man like Marcus King. As I know you I've been detailed to pick over the pieces — we should be able to work together without friction. Agreed?'

'Sure. You know what happened?'

'I've read the report. How about you filling in the details?'

'We're still trying to dig them out.' Markham led the way towards the sheeted figure. 'Elgar,' he explained. 'One of King's guards. He was on duty when it happened.' He stooped and lifted the sheet. Beneath lay a charred mess of torn and lacerated flesh and clothing. 'He managed to get his boss to a drop-shaft — probably threw him into the opening, then caught the full force of the blast.' He dropped the sheet back over the body.

'Drop-shaft?' Steve raised his eyebrows. 'Where does it lead?'

'To a bomb-proof in the lower levels.'

'An emergency exit.' The agent looked at the ruined luxury of the room. 'Now why should a man like King want a thing like that?'

'Why should he be guarded day and night?' Markham shrugged. 'Maybe he's scared stupid of assassination. Or maybe he's afraid of fire. I wouldn't know.'

'You're a liar,' said Steve evenly. 'But, from the look of it, his precautions were justified. My guess is that he beat the old man with a scythe by the skin of his teeth. Have you asked him about it?'

'No.' Markham stepped back as two men came to collect the body. They looked at him and he nodded, his eyes following the stretcher as it left the room. 'Not yet. You don't ask a man like King anything until he's ready to be asked. At the moment he's under sedation — or so I was told.'

'It can wait. Any other casualties?'

'Two.' Markham was grim. 'The boys in the helijet. They must have seen the plane coming and tried to deflect it. They died trying.'

Steve nodded, sympathizing with the acid in the chief's voice, then crossed the room to the shattered window. He stood looking through the jagged opening, feeling the tug of the wind, then glanced to where the men worked at the far end of the room. The plane was almost buried in the structure of the wall that had taken the main force of the impact. He frowned and looked again through the window.

'Something on your mind, Steve?' Markham had joined him.

'Just a thought. What do you make of it?'

'Isn't it obvious? Some crazy idiot flying too fast and too low. He lost control and — ' The chiefs thumb jerked expressively over his shoulder. He caught Steve's expression as he turned. 'You doubt it?'

'I'm thinking about it. Wouldn't a man in a plane do his best to avoid an obstruction like this building?'

'Sure. But if he's lost control what could he do about it?'

'He could try something. No plane ever gets that much out of control.' Steve paused, thinking about it, then shook his head. 'Something's wrong here. Unless the pilot were dead or unconscious he would have tried something. If the witnesses are correct it came in fast and low and straight towards the building. If it hadn't been for that heli deflecting it — '

'King would be dead,' snapped Markham. 'Nothing living in this room could have survived a direct impact. He was lucky. Two good men died to give him that luck. Well, it happens.'

'Yes,' said Steve thoughtfully. 'It happens — to people like King.'

A technician called from the group working at the wrecked plane. 'Hey, Chief, do you want to take a look at this?'

They had freed the pilot. Steve watched as the photographers recorded the scene, looking dispassionately at the broken body, the unrecognisable face. A metal circlet girdled the skull.

'Hold it,' he snapped as a man stooped to remove it. The technician looked his surprise.

'It's only a krown.'

'Maybe, but treat it with caution just the same.' He looked at Markham, not wanting publicly to override his authority. 'I'd like a report on that, Chief. Fast.'

'O.K, see to it, Hewitt.' Markham stepped back as the man carefully removed the circlet then snapped orders at the rest of his crew. 'Right. Get his prints. Send them to Central Registry. Get a retinal if you can. No? Well get his blood-type and do what you can with the rest.' He looked at the technician who had called him over. 'Have you, anything else, Eisten?'

The man looked at Steve.

'You can talk freely,' snapped Markham impatiently. He stepped further away from the men clustered about the body. 'What have you found?'

'Nothing unexpected.' Eisten had a thin, high-pitched voice that suited his arid manner. 'The plane was a normal commercial job, a sports model three years old. It had been fitted with extra rocket boosters and stripped for speed.'

'A hot rod,' said Markham. 'Anything else? Numbers? Markings?'

'All there. Tracing the crate will be simple.'

'Naturally,' said Steve dryly. 'You won't have any trouble identifying the pilot either. Was there any remote control?'

'No.'

'Are you certain?'

'I'm positive.' Eisten was offended. He continued his report, speaking directly to Markham. 'As far as I can tell there was no mechanical failure but a fuller report will have to wait until after laboratory analysis.'

'Naturally,' said the chief. 'Conclusions?'

'An accident. One of those things. The pilot could have had a blackout. It's anyone's guess.'

Markham nodded dismissal then looked at Steve.

'Well? You heard the man?'

'I heard him,' said Steve, 'but what else did you expect it to look like? If the plane had carried no markings or had been gimmicked in some way it would have yelled suspicion. But your man is wrong. It was no accident.'

'Trying to make work, Steve?'

'No, but I'm not running away from the facts either. Where's the man who is working on that krown?'

Hewitt had finished his examination. He came towards them at Markham's call, the circlet swinging from his hand. He looked at Steve with respect.

'You were right,' he said. 'This thing was booby-trapped. Explosive and thermite both.'

'Why didn't it blow?' Markham watched as Steve took the circlet from the technician. Hewitt shrugged.

'A freak. It had a kinetic fuse of some kind. A neat idea but it didn't work.'

'And if it had?'

'It would have melted itself down into scrap.'

Curiosity sparkled in the technician's eyes. 'Now why would a man wear a krown fitted with a thing like that?'

'Maybe he liked living dangerously,' said Steve. 'Who can tell what goes on in a kink's mind?'

'Has a kink got a mind?' said Hewitt.

He left and Steve led Markham away

from his men, down to the far end of the room. He held up the circlet, his mouth set in distaste. Crashing sounds came from the region of the wrecked plane. He ignored them.

'All right, Dale,' he said. 'Now we know. This was no kink-act and it was no accident either. This was a deliberate attempt at murder.'

'Are you sure?' Markham's voice was tight with anger. He was thinking of the two policemen who had died.

Steve nodded. 'I'm sure. Someone wanted King dead. Let's find out more about it.'

★ ★ ★

The pilot's name was Quentin Murray, 34 years old, married, no children, no evidence of disease, not wanted by the authorities. Unemployed for four years. Now dead.

'A kink.' Markham dropped the flimsy from Central Registry on his desk. It was late afternoon and he was looking tired. 'Nothing to do, nothing to hope for, nothing to be proud of. So he dived at the Palace. A regular kink trick.'

'If the krown had blown it would have looked an accident,' said Steve sourly. 'Now it looks like a kink-act. Whoever is behind it has brains as well as money.'

He leaned back in his chair, only half-aware of the bustle beyond the transparent partition; the seeming chaos of the local police headquarters. Through a window he could see the soaring tower of the Palace. He looked at it. Markham followed his gaze.

'Get anything?'

'No. King is under sedation. King is going to stay that way.' Steve turned from the window. 'I've checked the commercial situation. There have been no massive transfers of stock; no financial manoeu-vring. If King is getting ready to expand his empire then he's doing it without trace.'

'How about the others?'

'The same. All negative. His competitors are apparently satisfied to maintain the *status quo*.'

'They wouldn't have tried assassination

anyway,' said Markham. 'Their killings are done on the market. Their idea of destroying a man is to ruin him. They don't like outright murder — it could backfire.'

Markham sounded confident but Steve knew better. To be a tycoon a man had to be strong and, to such personalities, the use of force held a certain appeal. He looked up as Eisten entered the office. The technician held a sheaf of papers. He dropped them on the desk.

'There are the lab reports, Chief. The plane was a sporter, converted six months ago and licensed for private sky only. It was mechanically sound at the time of the crash.' He gestured towards the papers. 'You want to check?'

Markham shook his head. 'So it was pilot-failure then? Nothing else?'

'Nothing. The plane was registered to the Skyburner's Circus. They're at the Freedrome at the — '

'All right,' said Markham. 'I know where it is.'

The Freedrome was a garbage-filled quarry at the edge of town. A circle of vision-baffles lined the perimeter and posters screamed the attractions of the circus. Empty cartons, wrappers and discarded betting tickets littered the dirt. Past a line of weathered hangars stood an uneven row of caravans. Markham led the way to one of the largest, rang the bell, waited. The door opened and a man looked out.

'Are you Judd Klien?'

'That's right.' The man's eyes were cool, speculative.

'Who wants him?'

'Police.' Markham flashed his badge and pushed his way into the caravan. Steve followed him. The circus owner hesitated then closed the door. He was cautious.

He waited for Markham to speak.

'You own a plane,' said the chief. 'Registered number 243PSO 564S. Tell mc about it.'

'I already have,' said Klien. 'Where is it?' He looked at the two men, the comers of his eyes crinkling as if amused. 'I reported it stolen over an hour ago. Isn't that what you've called about?'

Markham looked his surprise.

'Let me get this straight,' he said evenly. 'You say that the plane was stolen about an hour ago?'

'I reported it then,' corrected the circus owner. 'I don't know when it was lifted. Sometime early morning, I guess. We found it missing when it was due to go on test.' He saw the look of disbelief on Markham's face. 'I guess you don't know the score. We get plenty of engine noise and some of the pilots test their crates at peculiar times. So it doesn't signify all that much when a plane takes to the air. I reported the loss as soon as I heard of it. That's all I can say.'

'Are you sure about that?'

'Sure I'm sure.' Klien's eyes were steady as he looked at the chief. 'Have you found it yet?'

'We found what was left of it.'

'Damaged?'

'It's a wreck. Who took it?'

'Now how the hell would I know that? We get all kinds. Sightseers, buffs, kinks, would-bes and has-beens. Maybe some junked-up kid figured himself as a pilot. If

29

you've got him you should know.' Klien looked at a table, bearing a bottle and glasses. 'Want a drink?'

Markham shook his head. 'Do you know a man named Murray?'

'Never heard of him. Did he steal my plane?'

'He flew it. He's dead. Are you sure you never heard of him? Maybe he wanted a job as a pilot.'

'Who doesn't?' Klien poured himself a drink. He looked at Steve who shook his head. Picking up the glass he sat down. 'I get them all the time. Warn them of high-G and they laugh. Tell them it takes more than wishing to make the grade and they sneer. Ask them for cash and they run.'

'All of them?'

'Not all. Some of the rich kids pay for a crack. I hire them a plane and let them enter the preliminaries. The boys usually let them gain the edge. They lose it before morning.'

'And their money too, is that it?'

'Why not?' Klien shrugged at Markham's expression. 'If a man wants to back himself who am I to stop him?' Abruptly he swallowed his drink, slammed down the glass, jerked to his feet. 'All right. You've had your say. Now get out of here and let me work.'

'One last thing.' Steve stepped forward before Markham could speak. 'The plane you lost, did you win that on a bet?'

'How did you guess?' Klien poured himself another drink. 'Some rich kid fancied himself and didn't trust my planes. So he used his own. He lasted three races and lost his shirt, his ship and some skin.' He narrowed his eyes. 'You want to make something out of it?'

'Did I say so?'

'You don't have to say. You cops are all alike. Well, to hell with you. I pay my taxes and stay clean. Now get out of here and let me earn a living!'

★   ★   ★

Outside Steve looked thoughtfully at the hangars and workshops. The scream of tested engines tore the air and a plane, exhaust baffled, soughed in a tight circle

31

overhead. A second joined it and they flew in close manoeuvre, wings almost touching, diving, separating when it seemed they must surely crash.

'Clever,' said Steve. 'Those pilots know how to handle a plane.'

'They should. They're experts.' Markham glanced back at the caravan. 'So's Klien.'

'You think that he was lying?'

Markham shrugged and led the way back to the official car. Talking was easier when the vehicle had carried them from the scream of tested engines.

'It would have been easy for Murray to have taken the plane,' said Steve. 'Even if the loss had been reported at once it would have made no difference. The person steering him didn't intend for Murray to come back.'

'Klien reported the loss to cover himself,' said Markham. 'He knows more than he's told.'

'Perhaps. Maybe he knows Murray, maybe not, but one thing is certain. Whoever was behind Murray knew about the circus. And there's the plane. It was worth any three of the others. I doubt if

Klien ever intended to race it — he would have been a fool if he had.'

'Are you saying that it was a plant?'

'I doubt it. It seems a little too obvious and you can trace it back without trouble. Our quarry is too smart to leave such a connection. But that plane was there for a purpose. My guess is that it wasn't for regular racing. So what was it doing there?'

'Maybe Klien was holding it to see?'

'Maybe. You can find out. But someone knew of it and steered Murray to it. It was the one best suited to his purpose.'

'So it comes back to the circus.' Markham scowled at the impassive back of the uniformed driver. 'Damn the luck! Of all the close-mouthed crews circus folk are the worst. They'll cover for each other all the way. Whoever steered Murray knew what they were doing. Clever! Damned clever!'

'Not so clever,' reminded Steve. 'The krown didn't blow. It should have done. It gives us a lead.'

'You're working on it?'

'I'm waiting for the lab reports. In the

33

meantime look up Murray's wife. You know where she is?'

'Wait a minute.' Markham picked up a handset spoke into it, waited. He looked at Steve over the mouthpiece. 'I'm still going to trace that plane. There's a chance that — ' He broke off, listened, snapped a question, listened again. He replaced the instrument.

'I've saved you a journey. I had a check made on Murray's wife. Little Stella isn't at home. She hasn't been home all night.'

3

The man was tall, dark, blue-eyed. He had a hard cruel mouth, a strong jaw, small ears set close to his cropped skull. His clothes were expensive, his hands well-kept, his manner alert.

'Ransom,' said Markham. 'David Ransom.' He watched the man on the screen. Superimposed lettering gave relevant information. 'Stella Murray's boy-friend — or one of them. We found them at North Polar.'

Steve nodded. He was intent on the man portrayed on the screen. He was speaking, the voice cultured and with an underlay of mockery. Markham pressed a button and the scene changed.

'Watch this.'

It was the same man but now he was naked aside from snug briefs, his body warm with the sheen of oil. The ten-inch knife in his hand glittered like an icicle. He held it with professional competence.

The blue eyes were narrowed, gleaming with a killer's light. He moved forward, poised on the balls of his feet.

'Dave Ransom,' said Markham again. 'He's a knife-fighter and a good one. Not that he goes into the ring personally now. He handles promotions, runs a string, arranges bouts on the Free Circuits.'

'Promotions?' Steve was thoughtful.

'You get the connections?' Markham nodded. 'He could get hold of a gimmicked krown. I thought of that but he checks out clean. He and Stella left the city before midnight and arrived at North Polar three hours before the crash. They stayed there until we found them. Call it thirty-six hours. They give each other a cast-iron alibi.' He anticipated Steve's question. 'It's genuine. I've checked the resort and there's no doubt about it. Neither could have been personally involved.'

'That doesn't mean that they are innocent,' said Steve. 'The thing could have been fixed. What about the woman?'

'Stella?' Markham shrugged. He pressed another button. A woman stared at them.

She was pretty in a hard, artificial way. Her voice tended to be shrill. Her body was beautiful.

Steve recognised the type.

'A girl with too much ambition and not enough of what it takes,' said Markham. 'She married Murray when he was working — my guess is that she wanted a regular meal-ticket. When he hit the skids she looked around.'

'Why didn't he divorce her?'

'Why should he?' Markham was cynical. 'He couldn't get a better looker and divorce costs money. Maybe he was content with the crumbs.' He hit the release. 'Forget her. She hasn't any brains outside of the bedroom. I don't know what Ransom saw in her.'

'She was Murray's wife,' pointed out Steve. 'There's a connection.'

'It could be coincidence. I told you — she played around.' His voice changed. 'But here's another connection. Ransom knows King.'

'A knife fighter?'

'He wasn't always that. King picked Ransom out of the gutter when he was just a kid. He gave him an education, treated him almost like a son — and then, for some reason, he threw him back into the gutter. That was five years ago.'

Steve was interested. 'What happened to him? Ransom, I mean?'

'He hit bottom. He'd been turned into a spoiled kid and had to learn fast.' Markham shrugged. 'I'll say this for him; he wanted to survive. Cheap fights, some fixing, you know how it is. He climbed fast. But I'll bet he thinks of King every time he sees his scars.'

'Revenge?' Steve considered it. 'After so long? Possible but I doubt it.'

'But it's a connection,' insisted Markham. 'Murray's wife, access to a gimmicked krown, a motive. It's a gift.'

'Yes,' said Steve dryly. 'Too much of a gift — but he has an alibi.'

* * *

The architect who had designed the display on the Palace had boasted that it couldn't be ignored. Linda Sheldon agreed with him.

BE A KING — WEAR A KROWN!

A promise and a command repeated three and a half times a second in a pulsating rhythm which gave the appearance of continuity but which was loaded with subliminal impact.

BE A KING — WEAR A KROWN!

She hated the very sight of it.

'Damn you to hell!' she said to the sign and covered the window with heavy curtains. They were old fashioned but they did their job. They cut out the night and the glare of the sign.

She crossed the room, a slightly-built woman m her late twenties, halting beside a wide desk. The top lifted as she touched a switch, the ranked tools and instruments lifting from beneath with a pneumatic sigh. A chair yielded beneath her weight. Adjusting goggle-magnifiers she concentrated on her work.

She was adapting a krown. It was fine, delicate work requiring both skill and concentration. The doorbell rang five times before it registered.

Steve smiled at her when she opened the door.

'Miss Sheldon?' He displayed his identification. Beneath the smile he was alert but her reaction was negative. She betrayed none of the guilt-symptoms usually created at the sight of the credentials.

'What do you want?' Her voice was cool, assured.

'Some help and information.' He looked past her into the big room. The desk looked normal; she had returned the workbench to its hiding place. 'May I come in?'

'Can I refuse?'

'Certainly — but why should you?' His smile remained as he stepped into the room. 'Can't we have a nice, friendly talk?'

'Under duress?' She shrugged with irritation. 'You are interrupting me. I do not like to be interrupted but I suppose that I have no choice in the matter.' She closed the door, walked into the room. 'Well, what do you want?'

'Some coffee,' he said blandly. 'Hot and black and strong.' He smiled at her expression. 'You did ask me,' he reminded. 'Do you mind?'

'For taking me so literally?' The calm effrontery of his request had appealed to her sense of humour. She thawed, returned his smile, gestured towards a chair. 'No, I don't mind. Ten minutes?'

It was ready in three and Steve examined the room as he sipped the coffee. It was good coffee. It was an expensive room.

'You are probably wondering at the reason for my visit,' he said as he set down the empty cup. 'For that you can blame Central Registry.'

'Shedding responsibility, Mr. Delmonte?'

'No, I'm stating a fact. You see we have a problem. We took all the factors that we think could help us and fed them into the computer. Your name was returned.'

'The problem?'

'It has to do with a krown,' he said casually. 'A very special krown. It had been adapted.'

He sensed the slight tension of her body. 'You think that I can help you?'

'Central Registry says that you can. You are a qualified electronician specialising in micro-currents and miniaturisation.

You graduated at the top of your class taking physics and metallurgy as associated subjects. You have also studied the electro-potential of the cortex with particular emphasis on the thalamus.'

'So?'

'So I would like you to tell me about krowns.'

'I see.' She rose with a smooth, lithe movement and crossed to the window. Savagely she jerked back the curtains. Outside the sign on the Palace made the night hideous with its glare. 'If you want to know about krowns,' she said bitterly, 'you should ask King.'

'I've tried. For a man who was almost killed by one of his own products he isn't very communicative.' Her face was turned from him; her expression hidden. 'You know about the crash?'

'The plane that hit the Palace. Yes. They said it was an accident.'

'It wasn't. The pilot was wearing an adapted krown.' He rose and joined her before the window. Reaching out he drew the curtains. 'Tell me about them.'

'They are based on the McKee effect.

A certain pattern of micro-radiation impinging on the cortex, and producing mental and physical reaction. But you must know this!'

'Yes,' he admitted. 'I know of the principle behind the krowns. What I want you to tell me is how they can be used for murder.'

He sensed the tension of her body again, the sudden catch of her breath, then she was moving across the room towards the chairs. Sitting down she poured herself more coffee. 'Want some?'

'Please.' He sipped while she spoke. He admired her self-possession.

'Take sleep,' she said abruptly. 'McKee found that if the wave-pattern of the brain as determined by the electro-encephalograph could be artificially produced and super-imposed on the cortex then the results were predictable. Sleep produces a certain wave-pattern. Reproduce it, superimpose it — and the patient would fall asleep. A quick, natural sleep that would last as long as the stimulus was applied. The application was obvious.'

'Artificial sleep,' he said. 'For as long as

the doctor considered necessary. Krowns replaced anaesthetics. A patient falls asleep and wakes healed. Intravenous feeding takes care of bodily nourishment. And?'

'It's the old story.' She sounded tired, depressed, more than a little disgusted. 'Sleep isn't the only reaction possible with a krown. Other wave-patterns can be copied. The entire spectrum of human emotion can be synthesised and applied. Need I stress the commercial application?'

They had replaced a host of drugs. Tranquillizers, stimulants, anti-depressants — the owner of a krown needed none of them. They could avoid depression, anger, shame. They had no need to feel inferior. They had no cause to experience fear.

A touch of a switch and a man would fall asleep — a built-in trip cutting the stimulus at any predetermined interval. Pay a little more and your krown would be fitted with extra attachments. You could feel euphoria, the titivation of the senses, pleasure, anticipation, desire . . . The limit was only what you could afford.

'Zombies!' She rose and paced the

floor. 'That's what krown-users are. They don't feel real, natural emotion at all. They merely respond like a frog's leg kicking to a jolt of current.' She shuddered. 'Can you imagine being made love to by a man wearing a krown?'

'No.'

'A woman, then. She'd want you because of the band around her head. You or any man. She wouldn't feel love, only lust. Remove the krown and would she feel the same? You'd never know. Thanks to King!'

'You don't like him?'

'No.' She met his eyes, her own oddly penetrating in their unwavering direct-ness. 'I detest him for the thief that he is.'

He waited, knowing that there had to be more.

'He stole the McKee effect. His lawyers moved in and, when it was over, he owned the basic discovery and all the relevant patents. He grew richer while McKee died in poverty. King!' She spat the word like an insult.

'You hate him?'

'Yes!'

'Enough to kill him?'

'Enough to wish him dead.' Her eyes were defiant. 'Is that what you came to find out?'

'No. You were telling me about the krowns.' He rose and stood beside the desk, his fingers running over the polished surface. 'Adapted krowns,' he reminded. 'The illegal ones.'

His knuckles made a drumming sound on the desk. A hollow sound.

She sighed and moved past him and he caught the delicate scent of perfume; the clean, feminine smell of cosmetics and womanliness.

'Call the brain a receiving set and the krown a broadcasting unit,' she said flatly. 'Now think of the reverse. A krown can be adapted to pick up and transmit the wave-pattern of a brain. In such a cases the wearer of a tuned krown will sense, feel, experience the same as wearer of the master does. Vicarious participation to the ultimate degree.'

'I see.' His hand left the desk as he moved closer to her. 'What is a matched pair?'

'Exactly what it says. Each krown acts

as both receiver and broadcaster. Each wearer experiences the other's emotions on a mounting, feedback cycle. They are popular with lovers; especially those with transvestite tendencies.'

'I can imagine,' he said dryly. 'And a master/slave control?'

'I don't know anything about that.'

'No?' His voice hardened. 'Then how is it that your thesis dealt with that particular subject?'

'My thesis dealt with problematical applications of the McKee effect,' she said coldly. 'I suggest you read it before making such broad statements.'

'I have.' He had surprised her. 'Let me tell you about them. About the krown Murray was wearing. It was a slave control. Someone, somewhere, wore the master. He saw through the pilot's eyes, guided the plane with his hands, dived to his death. Murray's death, not the one wearing the master. He was safe. Have you ever adapted a krown?'

The question caught her off-balance as he had intended.

'I — '

'Have you?'

'Isn't that against the law?'

'Not if it is done for the purpose of legitimate research. What do you do for a living?'

'I — ' Anger dusted her cheeks, sparkled in her eyes. 'That is my business.'

'No,' he corrected sharply. 'Mine. I represent Security. You are listed as a self-employed consultant. Is that correct?'

'Yes.'

'Who are your customers?'

'Businesses, people, anyone who wants and can pay for my skill.'

'Fight promoters?' His voice was a club beating at her self-control. 'The sharks on the Free Circuit who can afford to pay for gimmicked krowns? Is that who you work for?'

Her anger was a shield he couldn't penetrate. Abruptly his voice softened. 'Do you know a man named Murray? Klien? Ransom?' He listed the names as she shook her head. He handed her a photograph. 'Have you ever seen this man?'

'No.' She was definite. 'Who is he?'

'Ransom. Tell me, why do you hate King?'

'I told you.'

'No. You said that you despised him for wrongs done to another in the past. That is not a strong enough reason to wish him dead. Not for an intelligent woman.'

She didn't answer.

'You have another reason,' he insisted. 'Tell me.'

She crossed the room. The curtains made a sharp, swishing sound as she drew them back. She looked towards the Palace, the sign staining her face with its garish light.

'I hate King because I'm afraid of him. Afraid of what he can do. What I know he can do. If you are as concerned about Security as you say than you should give whoever tried to kill him a medal.'

She turned and looked at him, her eyes bitter.

'So don't ask me to help you to find them.'

4

The room was a conical simulacrum of a Caribbean Paradise. From the high apex an artificial sun shone over living murals. Gaudy birds flitted among exotic vegetation. The soft susurration of a distant sea hung on the scented air.

Marcus Edward King was not impressed.

The room was a toy, the product of electronic genius, coupled with the power of wealth. Once it had amused him to control his environment with the flick of a finger.

'You must relax.' Fullen's fingers probed expertly at the base of Marcus's neck. 'The psychic trauma of your escape is stronger than you think. It should not be ignored.'

Marcus grunted his irritation. 'I'm not ignoring it.'

'I speak in a medical sense. You're a mass of tension. You should take a week of deep-sleep.'

'Fool!'

The fingers hesitated, hardened, dug a fraction deeper. Marcus snarled like a wolf.

'Someone has tried to kill me and you tell me to go to sleep! Is that what you call good advice?'

'In your case — yes.'

'Why? What makes me so special?'

'You are not alone. You can relax without fear. You have others to protect you. You — '

'Protect!' Marcus swung from the couch and glared at the doctor. 'Where was that protection when I needed it most?'

Fullen remained calm.

'Elgar saved your life.'

'So what? He was a guard. He was paid to do a job. He did it — just.' Impatiently Marcus snatched his robe higher about his neck. 'The fact remains that I was almost killed. Killed! And you tell me to go to sleep!'

Impatiently he strode the floor. The soft decor mocked his mood. He sensed it and pressed a button. The mural swirled, steadied into a new pattern. Barred and pointed windows looked onto a checker-board countryside over which wended colourful figures. The walls became granite, hung with weapons, bright with trophies. The carpet changed to the colour of stone.

The king was in his castle, thought Fullen and wondered if Marcus guessed how easily he had betrayed himself. He was afraid and had surrounded himself with archaic defences.

'You wanted to kill me,' said Marcus suddenly. 'Why?' He stared at the impassive face of the doctor. 'Your hands betrayed you,' he snapped. 'I felt their pressure. Your fingers were on the carotids. Three minutes and I would have been dead.'

'No,' said Fullen.

'You deny it?'

'I am your physician,' said Fullen evenly. 'I am a psychiatrist. I accept your insults for what they are. The expressions of a man in fear.'

'I have a right to be afraid.' Marcus lifted a hand to his throat. 'So vulnerable,' he whispered. 'A man is so vulnerable. Do you ever think of that?'

'Consciously, no. My profession is to save life not think of ways to take it. May we end this subject of conversation?'

'It bothers you?'

'Paranoia bothers me,' said Fullen quietly. 'You refuse to admit the importance of psychosomatic stress. A man in perpetual fear is in a condition of continued physical tension. Such a state, unless alleviated, is dangerous. It is wearing to the young — it can kill the old.'

'I see,' said Marcus. He bared his teeth. 'Are you saying that my mental state is abnormal?'

Fullen didn't answer.

'Get out!'

* * *

Marcus sat and stared at the walls of his make believe castle, half-wishing that he had been born in another place, another time. Almost at once he dismissed the notion for the absurdity that it was. He had no time for fancies.

Time! There wasn't enough time!

He found and pressed a button. A face appeared on a screen. Fromarch blinked as he recognized his caller.

'Why, Mr. King, sir. This is an unexpected pleasure!'

Marcus ignored the pleasantry.

'What is the finalised figure on the saturation sales index of the proposed new model?'

'Model Z?' Fromarch was uncomfortable but he managed to retain his smile. 'I'm afraid that you're a little early for that, Mr. King. We don't have it yet. The data is still in the machines.'

'How long?'

'Well — ' The smile grew even more strained. 'We should have it for you by tomorrow. Yes, sir, tomorrow for certain.'

'Tomorrow is twenty-four hours away,' snapped Marcus. 'Twenty-four hours wasted. Why the delay?' He didn't wait for an answer. 'Never mind. Transfer me to Perlew.'

Perlew was Head of Personnel, Technical Division.

'Yes, Mr. King?'

'Fromarch is behind schedule. Check and find out if he's been dragging his feet. If he has fire him.' The screen blanked out. For a moment Marcus hesitated, his fingers resting on the buttons, then withdrew his hand. That wasn't the answer . . . Tiredly he leaned back, looking at the pointed windows, the sun-dappled scene beyond. Life had been simple in those days when the barons ruled and science leaned towards magic. But the same human motives still held. Greed and hate and fear with the rack and dungeons below and, is the turret, the men of genius striving to unlock the secrets of the ages. No longer to make gold — he could do that easily enough. But to find things far more precious.

Life and the secrets of life, so that those who had could hold.

They could find it, too, given the time. Time!

He rose and crossed the room. A panel slid open. He stepped into the cage of an elevator and dropped down . . . down,

down. In this age the turrets were buried deep.

A man met him as he left the cage. The air was cool, sterile, tainted with the smell of antiseptics. Marcus shivered. He had been too impatient to dress. Not that it mattered.

'Do you want to look over the labs, Mr. King?' Gilder was polite but he could not avoid displaying a little impatience. Marcus was not offended. He was impatient himself.

'Yes.'

'Then if you will please shower and change — ?'

It was routine. Silently he allowed the jets to drench him with antiseptics, the hot air to dry him, the dispenser to eject soft, shapeless clothing still warm from the ovens.

Dressed, clean, less irritable now that he was doing something positive, he followed the scientist into the laboratories. Men worked in silent concentration. Caged animals looked from the walls. Glass and metal shone bright in the artificial daylight.

'Progress?'

'As expected, Mr. King.' Gilder led the way to where animals lived in hermetically sealed glass. 'We're running the last of the tests of the present series. Fifteen hundred specimens to be exact.' He tried a little humour. 'It's lucky that rats are so inexpensive.'

'Never mind that! Are they the best medium?'

'No, but they are the most convenient.' Gilder dared to smile. 'We can hardly use men.'

In the old days they would have used men.

'You said that this was the last of the present series,' said Marcus. 'Has the new serum proved successful?'

'Yes — to a limited degree. The residual cholestrol is completely removed and with less physical shock than previous methods but there is no tremendous difference in observable lifespan. We are, of course, using aged specimens.'

Marcus nodded. He was not interested in extending the lives of young men.

'Mallory is investigating the effects of

controlled radiation on the pineal. We still don't know what is the exact purpose of this gland but he suspects that . . . ' The voice droned on, Marcus listening but not wholly understanding. It didn't worry him. He was not a scientist. He bought scientists. ' . . . an ambitious programme. At a guess I'd say he'd need at least five hundred Rhesus monkeys but the expense — '

'Buy them.'

'Five hundred, Mr. King?'

'A thousand if you need them.'

How much was life worth?

A second laboratory led from the first. A trapped passage, a barrier between them. A different laboratory with not much glass and little metal but ranked machines and hair-fine instruments. And animals. Plenty of animals.

Gilder halted behind a technician. The man was stooped over an elaborate krown.

'We're managing to get almost total master/slave control,' said Gilder enthusiastically. 'Not only visual and aural reception but emotional and tactile as well. Four of the five senses, Mr. King, and a large part of the emotional spectrum!'

'What's the missing sense?'

'Taste. We're having trouble with that one. When we solve it, it will be possible for a man really to live by proxy.'

'And die by proxy?'

Gilder lost some of his enthusiasm.

'That's a part of the trouble, Mr. King. If we get too close an affinity then there seems to be an actual merging of the personalities. In such a case the traumatic shock of death could be transmitted with unfortunate results.' He hesitated. 'In fact we've had a couple of rather scary incidents. Dogs were used as the slaves, of course, and trained operators the masters. When a close degree of affinity had been reached we killed the animals while still in circuit.'

'What happened?'

'In one case catatonia of the operator. In the other amnesia. Both, fortunately, responded to treatment.' Gilder pulled thoughtfully at his ear. 'The trouble is obviously psychological. It will have to be solved before we can hope to experiment with the higher animals.'

Marcus nodded. He had expected nothing different. They had been faced with the same problem for years.

'We're trying a new approach on the transference of wave-patterns,' said Gilder. 'We've had some degree of success. The trouble is that . . . '

There was always trouble. Little things which made the apparently obvious the impossible to attain. Things like the subduing of the host personality, the impossibility of recording a true pattern — the machines allowed too high a margin of error, the difficulty of finding compatible types for experiments. It was all compromise and promise.

Promise!

He could not live on promises.

Gilder halted beside a seated compartment. A dog lay within, a mesh of wires sprouting from its skull. Tubes led into the wall of its chest. Its eyes were closed. It didn't move. An adapted krown rested on the shaven head.

'This is interesting,' said Gilder. 'This dog is, physically, dead. We're keeping it alive by mechanical means. Keeping its brain alive, I should say, but that's nothing new. The use of mechanical hearts, lungs, stomachs has been known for years, We have gone a step further. The dog is in affinity with that one over there.' He pointed to where a canine crouched in a cage. 'Now watch.'

He turned and spoke to the operator. The man nodded and rested his hands on a panel.

'Bark,' he said. The other dog barked.

'Walk to the left. The right. Squat. Scratch side of head. Sit up and beg.'

Like an echo the dog followed the commands.

Marcus raised his eyebrows.

'It isn't obeying voice-commands,' explained Gilder. 'The appropriate stimuli are fed into the brain of the dog in the compartment — dog A. Dog A is in krown circuit with dog B. A thinks — or is forced to do the equivalent of thinking — and dog B performs the actions.

'So?' Marcus's voice was cold.

'It is an extreme solution,' admitted Gilder. 'But it is a solution. A man could be kept alive as we are keeping dog A. After all, what is really important about a man? His brain. Keep that alive and the man is alive. By use of a krown we can give him a complete proxy-life — provided we can find him a suitable host, of course.'

'Of course,' said Marcus. There was a peculiar ringing in his ears, a tension at his temples. 'He would have to have that.'

'In such a case his life could be extended indefinitely,' continued Gilder cheerfully. 'In — ' he broke off. 'Are you feeling unwell, Mr. King?'

'No. I'm all right.'

Marcus was curt but it was a lie. The thin ringing seemed to penetrate his skull and the band around his temples was crushing his brain. And there was something wrong with his eyes. The dog in the case was no longer a dog. It had changed, altered into something horribly familiar.

Into a grey face on a white pillow.

The grey death mask of his father.

'Mr. King!'

He smelt the stench of something acrid.

'Mr. King, sir!'

'I'm all right,' he said. 'I tell you that I'm all right!' He turned away from the case and what it contained.

It was alive.

It would continue to live.

But there had to be another way.

5

At eleven in the morning Ellen Langdy trudged down the corridor of the twenty-fifth floor of the hotel in which she had spent the past eighteen years of her life. She had been a chambermaid when she joined the staff, she was one now. She didn't let it bother her. At 52 she had other problems. Sam was one.

He was her only child and had been trouble from the day he was born. Now he was writing from the sea-farm. He'd signed on for the standard five-year term and now wanted to buy his contract. If she gave him the money she would be broke. If she didn't he was likely to make a run for it. If he did he would be caught and liable to the extreme penalty under the commercial code.

And he would be caught. She had no doubt of it.

She sighed, wishing that Joe was still around to advise her, then forced a smile as another of her problems came in sight. The supervisor glanced pointedly at her watch.

'You're late, Langdy,' she snapped. 'This floor should be finished by now.'

'I'm sorry, madam.' Experience had taught her never to argue. 'It's just that — '

'I don't want any excuses. Now hurry and finish your work.'

Number 2552 was holding her up. The occupant was still in his room and looked like staying there all day. That didn't matter but, if she didn't clean his room, he might complain. She decided to take a chance. He could be a good-natured one who wouldn't object. He could be a careless one. He could even be an understanding one.

He was neither. He was dead.

She called the desk and sat down to wait.

'H. S. Shiel,' said the hotel detective. He was a thin, worldly-wise man of 43 and nothing the guests of the Hotel Excel could do had the power to surprise him. 'Registered two days ago. Stayed close to his room. No obvious friends. Can you add anything to that, Ellen?'

'No, Mr. Hughes.'

He nodded, looking at the body in the chair, the bottle and glass on the table, the scattered clothes and the still-burning bedside lamp. It was his first duty to summon the police but duty is a relative term. Hughes was a practical man.

'All right, Ellen,' he decided. 'I'll handle this. Stay close and don't talk. Off you go now.'

Alone he moved quickly about the room, smelling the bottle and glass, examining the body with his eyes, searching the room. He disturbed nothing and was careful to leave no prints.

'Not a dutch,' he mused. 'Not unless he found a new way out.'

He stooped and examined the krown the dead man was wearing. It had cost more than the detective earned in a year. The pyjamas, robe and clothing were of high quality. Number 2552 was no pauper. He touched the flesh and found it cold.

'He must have kicked it last night,' Hughes decided. 'Came up here, ordered a bottle, or had one already in his room, changed, sat down for a final drink and — curtains!' He shrugged. 'Well, let's see what he carried.'

Methodically he began to search the dead man's effects. The bags held nothing unusual. In the breast pocket of a jacket he found a notebook. He opened it, frowned at the scrawl it contained, guessing that it was some kind of code or private shorthand. The wallet was more interesting. He pursed his lips at the sight of a wad of currency, then removed half of it. Half wouldn't be noticed. To take it all would be to arouse suspicion — to neglect the opportunity would be stupid.

Hughes was not a stupid man. His eyes narrowed at the sight of what else the wallet contained. It was an ornate identification/credit card bearing a photograph of the dead man together with relevant information. It was overprinted with a lustrous crown.

The late Mr. H. S. Shiel had belonged to the King Organisation.

Hughes smiled as he looked at the dead

man, feeling a hard, warm glow in the pit of his stomach.

'Hell,' he said softly. 'It's Christmas!'

*   *   *

An hour later he called the police. The autopsy took place that afternoon. The coroner sat the following morning. A report was sent as a matter of courtesy to the Palace and another to Dale Markham as Chief of Local Police in the Palace area. A third went to Security.

Steve learned of it as a matter of routine.

'One of King's boys,' said Markham. He dug out his copy of the report. 'Died down at Malibu sometime yesterday in the small hours. Midnight before last at the earliest. Heart.'

'Let me see that.' Steve read the report and felt the itching of suspicion. Shiel had been one of King's top men — the coincidence was worrying. Markham shrugged when he mentioned it.

'One way and another King employs

enough people to populate a small city. The odds are in favour of something happening to one of them when it happens to the boss. It's just a matter of statistical averages.'

'Maybe.' Steve wasn't convinced. 'I'm not satisfied. So little cash. So few effects. No apparent reason for being where he was. And the prognosis! Heart ceased to function. Damn it, why?'

'I don't know and I don't care.' Markham leaned back in his chair. 'I've enough to do trying to solve the big one without worrying about what happens outside of my jurisdiction.'

'Yours,' said Steve. 'But not mine. I'm going to check this out.'

A flyer took him to the airfield. A stratjet wafted him to Malibu. A helicab dropped him at the precinct of the Hotel Excel. A bored officer conducted him into the office of the local chief.

'Always ready to help Security,' he said when Steve had introduced himself. He was a plump man who radiated a cultivated bonhomie. 'What can I do for you?'

Steve told him. The chief lost some of his charm.

'Well now,' he said slowly. 'I can't quite see what you're after. We handled the matter to everyone's satisfaction and — '

'Not to mine,' Steve interrupted. 'That's why I'm here.' He said what he wanted to know. The chief shrugged.

'He didn't have a lot of cash but what would he want folding money for? His credit was good. Few effects? Maybe he liked to travel light. No, I don't know what he was doing in the area but I can guess. It's vacation country. Mr. Delmonte.'

'Who found him?'

'It's in the report. Ellen Langdy. She's the chambermaid. The hotel detective took over.'

'Both honest?'

'Well now.' The chief puffed out his cheeks. 'Let's just say that I've nothing against either of them. No record — if they had one they wouldn't be working at the Excel.'

The doctor was more informative. He looked at Steve from beneath bushy white eyebrows. An old man glad to be left alone.

'He died,' he said. 'His heart stopped beating. It happens.'

'It happens all the time,' said Steve coldly. 'What I want to know is why did it happen? What killed Shiel?'

'He died of natural causes.' The doctor shrugged at Steve's expression. 'What else can I say? He had a physical condition of which he was probably unaware. A rare but potentially dangerous complaint. He could have lived without treatment for another ten years. He was unlucky, that is all there is to it.'

'Not quite.' Steve looked thoughtfully at the doctor. He was old but seemed competent. 'Have you ever heard of a coagulator?'

'I have.' The doctor smiled with faint irony. 'I am the police surgeon,' he reminded. 'But Shiel was not murdered with such a weapon. The clot created by a coagulator has certain unmistakable characteristics. Such a clot was not present in the region of the heart. I'd stake my reputation on it.'

71

'You may have to,' said Steve. 'Is the body still here?'

'It is. We are holding it against instructions from his employer. He worked for Mr. King, you know.'

'I'm not impressed. Keep it here. Hold it for Security.'

'But if Mr. King — '

'Forget him. This is a Security matter. King can't have the body until we're through with it. So keep it in freeze. All of it.'

* * *

Outside Steve hesitated then walked over to the Hotel Excel. The manager shook his head.

'Hughes isn't here, Mr. Delmonte. He took off right after the inquest.'

'Do you know where he went?'

'No. He said he had things to do, wanted to advance his day off.' The manager shrugged. 'What be does in his own time is his own business.'

'All right,' said Steve. 'Where's his room?'

The room was one of the hotel's smaller apartments. A couple of simulated leather cases rested on top of the wardrobe. Steve searched them. He ran his hands over the two suits, slipped his fingers between the piles of underwear. A dresser yielded a heap of odds and ends, books, magazines, some travel folders. A half-filled box of small calibre cartridges stood in a box with a can of gun-oil and pull-through. Two spare clips were empty. A gas pencil with a broken valve had been tossed aside.

Steve dropped to his knees, stared at the bottoms of the drawers, the underside of the bed. A passbook caught his eye. He raised his eyebrows at the amount it showed. He rose and stood looking around the room. Then he picked up the phone.

'Operator? Did Hughes make any calls today? Outside calls?'

'No, sir.'

'Receive any? One? Local or long distance? I see. Thank you.'

He replaced the instrument and stood looking down at the table. Faint lines in the polish caught his eyes. He stooped, looking at them at an acute angle, taking care that his breath should not disturb the almost invisible film of dust. Again he lifted the phone.

'What time was this room cleaned today? I see. Do you know if Hughes caught a cab? Please find out. Yes, you can call back here.'

Again he stared at the faint marks on the table. A directory stood beneath the phone. He lifted it, riffled the pages, frowned at what he saw. The phone rang.

'Yes?' He listened to the operator's voice. 'Good. Yes. That's right, the same driver. I'll be right out.'

Hughes had taken a cab. He hadn't phoned for it but the driver knew him and had remembered.

'Picked me up halfway down the block,' he said as he guided the vehicle. 'Just flagged me down. I wouldn't have stopped but I know him.' He cursed softly to himself as he dodged a truck. 'Damn hogs,' he commented. 'They think they own the road.'

'Did he talk to you?'

'Just the usual gossip. Mostly about the inquest. Fancy finding a guy all cold like that?' The driver shook his head. 'Well, as I say, you never know.'

'No,' said Steve. 'Was he riding high?'

'Now you come to mention it, he was.' The driver swore again as a girl tried to commit suicide beneath his wheels. 'Crazy woman!' he yelled. He shook his head as the danger passed, then snapped his fingers. 'That reminds me — he gave me a tip. A fat one.'

'For what?'

'For — ' The driver grunted. 'Never mind.'

'Here.' Steve leaned forward, a note in his hand. The driver whistled.

'Five birds!'

'Keep talking. Did he stop anywhere? Give you anything to mail? To mind?' He showed his badge. 'It's O.K. I'm on his side.'

'No.' The driver's voice was flat. Steve recognised the barrier. He guessed that the man was telling the truth. Hughes wouldn't have been that careless. The cab stopped with a squeal of brakes. 'Here,' he said. 'This is the place.' Steve didn't move.

'Which way was he headed when you left him?'

'I didn't notice.' The driver turned. 'You want your money back?'

'No.'

The area was on the fringe beyond the polished centre, a maze of dilapidated houses scheduled for destruction. Giant machinery moved to one side in a cloud of dust. Faded shops looked like men who had long accepted defeat and now waited patiently to die.

Steve paused, remembering the address he had read traced on the polish of the table, faint in the dust. He halted, eyes narrowing at a self-serve shop, nodding as he saw a mailbox. A kid looked up at him, making a brave show in patched and faded jeans. His face bore the bloated look of substandard subsistence.

'Want to earn a bird?' Steve took the coin from his pocket. The kid almost swallowed his tongue in his eagerness to accept. 'You hang around here often?'

'Most days all day.' The kid was maybe

eleven with the bright eyes of youth and the knowing gleam of age.

'I'm looking for a man.' Steve described Hughes from his record card at the Hotel. 'He was headed towards the Dolman Place. Know it?'

'Sure.'

'Guide me for another five emus?'

Five Interplanetary Money Units would probably provide his food for a week — the kind of food he'd been reared on.

'Sure,' said the kid. 'This way, mister.'

The Dolman Place was just that, a place. Once it had been a square ringed with middle-income houses. There had been flowering trees and grass and maybe a pond. Now it was a broken, deserted slum. The air was thick with dust from the demolition machines, the ground shaking beneath their treads. Within a matter of days the area would be razed, the debris ready for fusing. New apartments would be built, a warren of low-income boxes reaching towards the sky. In weeks they would be fitted with the population overflow. In five years they would be another slum.

Steve halted on the edge of the ruined square. He looked at his guide.

'That one,' said the kid. He pointed to one of the terraced houses.

'O.K.,' said Steve. 'Beat it.'

The kid hesitated, dragging one foot in the dust.

'Go on,' snapped Steve. He waited until the kid had vanished back down the way they had come. Then he walked towards the house.

The door was gone, the windows glassless openings. He paused in the hall, sniffing at the air.

It was stale, acrid with the odour of shattered brick but clean of cigarette smoke, the smell of soap or alcohol.

Cautiously Steve searched the lower rooms. He climbed the stairs. Keeping close to the wall, and looked into the upper rooms. Nothing. He descended the stairs and stood looking thoughtfully at the hall. The dust bore recent traces. He turned and moved quietly towards the back door. A scrap of rubbish snapped beneath his foot in the backyard. He froze then moved towards the house on his left.

Something white showed in the dusty gloom of a back room.

It was Hughes. He was completely naked.

And completely dead.

6

The place had a gymnasium smell. A row of showers stood to one side, the stalls open. The paint was dark with age, the ceiling black with smoke, the faded prints on the walls mottled and stained.

Two men faced each other in the ring. They were naked aside from shorts and held practice knives in their hands. A third stood before a training device parrying the random slashes of a steel whip with a short bar of lead. Others went through routine exercises designed to speed reflexes and toughen muscle. The place was a normal appendage to the Free Circuit, duplicated a dozen times in the city, the hang-out of those with their eyes on the Mecca of the big time.

A man leaned against a wall and watched the fighters in the ring. They were scarred with the cicatrices of old wounds, white beneath the raw weals of recent training. The practice knives they held were edged with acid-soaked sponge.

'You want me?' Lou Benson, bald, fat, impatient, faced the stranger.

'You the owner?'

'That's right.'

'Nice pair of boys you've got there.' The stranger nodded towards the ring. 'You fighting them soon?'

'Maybe.' Lou narrowed his eyes at the man. He could be a casual buff, a tout for a promoter, a spy from an agent. He could be connected with the gambling syndicate looking for prospects to fix a match. He could be a kink.

He was none of these. He was an undercover man for the police.

'It'd be a nice match,' he said. He didn't look at Lou. 'In the raw, ten-inch blades, no quarter.' His breath made a sucking sound as he drew it between his lips. 'It'd be worth fifty birds for a ringside seat.'

'Buy yourself a ticket at any agency,' suggested Lou. 'Why waste money?'

He had nothing to worry about. Fights were legal. The Great Franchise gave a man the right to do what he wanted with his own body. But he was intrigued. He had met men like the stranger before. Kinks eager for a special thrill. Their eyes gave them away.

'You're kidding,' said the undercover man. 'Who's interested in Sunday-school stuff?' His eyes left the fighters and met those of the owner. 'I'd heard that you were a regular guy. One who could lay it on if the price was right. Get me?'

'I don't know what you're talking about.'

'No?' The stranger lifted a hand and flipped a finger against his forehead. 'Fifty birds to be in circuit on a death-bout. Seventy-five if I'm riding the guy who gets it. Can do?'

'You're crazy!' Lou's caution tempered his greed. Straight fights were legal but the use of adapted krowns was not. The wearer of such a krown was deemed to be under coercion. 'You've come to the wrong place, mister.'

'That's not how Ransom told it.' The stranger was annoyed. Saliva wet his lips and his eyes were wild. 'He said you could fix it and he's never steered me wrong before. What's the matter? The price too low?'

'Maybe.' Lou relaxed. 'You know Ransom?'

'Dave? Sure I do. I told you, he steered me this way. Check if you like.'

The owner checked as he knew he would. The answer was what he expected. Outside, well away from the gymnasium, the undercover man called the office on a public phone. Markham stared at him from the screen.

'Any luck?'

'No. I've tried seven different spots — all negative. If Ransom is around somewhere they don't know where he is. Want me to keep trying?'

'Yes, but don't make it obvious. If you get a lead let me know. Don't phone in for the sake of it. Cut.'

Markham scowled as the screen went blank. 'Well,' he said bitterly, 'that's another lesson in never taking anything for granted. Ransom's ducked surveillance.'

'How?' Steve looked up from a batch of reports. He looked tired. 'I thought that you had him covered.'

'We did.' Markham was sour. 'We had him tied and then he vanished.' He read the agent's expression. 'We got suckered by the oldest trick in the book,' he admitted. 'He switched in a ringer.'

'When was this?'

'Just after you left for Malibu. We followed him from his apartment. He ducked around for a while, entered an automat, went to the men's room. He came out, wandered around some more, took in a show and went home — we thought. A stranger walked out of his apartment — we let him go. We waited — no Ransom. We phoned — no answer. We made entry — no Ransom. We're still trying to find him.'

'A ringer,' said Steve thoughtfully. 'That's interesting.'

'Why so?'

'Premeditation. He had to have some-one with a similar build and colouring, wearing similar clothes and with a facsimile skin-mask all ready to make the switch. That took planning. How did he arrange it?'

Markham shrugged.

'Not by his own phone,' continued Steve, 'you had it tapped. By mail? No, too clumsy. Personal contact?' He looked at the chief. 'How about the woman?'

'Stella Murray? They don't see each other.'

'Any callers?'

'The usual. A mailman, a cleaner, a . . . ' Markham fumbled at his desk and found a report. 'A kid selling tv subscriptions. All genuine. I checked.'

'How did he travel?'

'By tube.'

'Did he make any outside calls?'

'One,' admitted Markham. 'He wasn't in the booth long enough for us to get it tapped.' He frowned at the agent. 'You think he arranged it then?'

'Maybe. Where was he heading when he made the switch?'

'As far as we can tell he was heading towards the Palace. His path was apparently aimless but the psych-boys swear that he was subconsciously driven in that direction.' Markham shook his head. 'And that makes them as crazy as coots.'

'I'm not so sure.' Steve looked thoughtfully at the spire of the Palace beyond the window of Markham's office. 'He had to have help to work the switch. Now, assuming that the switch wasn't his idea but that of someone else, who could that someone be?'

'Not King!' Markham was emphatic. 'I'll agree that he could have done it but I'll swear he didn't.'

'Why not?' Steve turned and looked at the chief. 'Because of what happened between them in the past? If King wanted Ransom he would have sent for him.'

'But Ransom wouldn't have gone to see King,' insisted the chief.

'You're wrong.' Steve smiled at the other's expression. 'If King had sent for him Ransom would have gone. He couldn't have helped himself. He would have had to go.'

'I can't see that.'

'Then you've still a lot to learn about human nature. The question is, why should King have sent for him at all?'

'I'll ask him that when we find him,' promised the chief. 'If King did send for him, that is. Personally I think that he had his own good reasons for wanting to vanish.'

'Such as?'

'We were too close for comfort. Ransom is no lily and he knows that we know it. My guess is that he couldn't stand for close investigation. Or his associates might have advised him to duck out of sight — or else. That would account for the smooth working of the switch.'

'Perhaps.' Steve was unconvinced.

'Or,' continued Markham casually, 'he was afraid of someone else. It could be that he is hooked up in the same way with the Sheldon woman.'

'Linda?' Steve frowned. 'The krowns?'

'What else?' To Markham it was obvious. 'Ransom must use them in his private promotions. He has to get them from somewhere. Sheldon adapts them. What more do you want?'

'Proof,' said Steve sharply. 'We don't know that she adapts krowns. You could make the same accusation against any other electronician. Why pick on her?'

For a long moment Markham didn't answer, then he shrugged. 'Coincidence,' he said quietly. 'They happen sometimes. Like Shiel dying down in Malibu. Had he been assassinated?'

'No.' Steve wondered why Markham had deliberately changed the subject. 'Shiel's death was as the autopsy stated. He died from natural causes. Hughes didn't.'

'The hotel detective,' Markham added. 'I read about that. Someone gave him a karate-chop to the neck. That's a regular deegee trick.'

'You think that's what it was?'

'Sure, it happens all the time,' said Markham. 'You get these gangs roaming the areas due for demolition — the dead areas. If anyone comes their way they lay for him. That's why Hughes was stripped when you found him. It's obvious what happened.'

'Too obvious.' Steve met the chief's eyes. 'That's what we're supposed to think. Hughes wasn't killed by a dead-gang. He was armed and no fool — he

88

wouldn't have let a deegee near him. He was killed by the person he went to meet.'

'And stripped?'

'And stripped?'

'He was selling something. The killer couldn't take the risk that he had it hidden in his clothing. So he stripped him just to make sure. The fact that stripping is a deegee trick was a bonus.' He paused. 'My guess is that he was blackmailing King.'

'Now I know you're crazy!' Markham snorted his contempt. 'What business would King have with a broken-down hotel dick?'

'Shiel.'

'What?'

'The answer is Shiel,' said Steve patiently. 'He was found dead almost an hour before Hughes notified the police. What was he doing during that hour? Hughes was hard put to it to scrape a living yet that same afternoon he paid a large sum of cash into his bank. Where did he get it from? Shiel had very little money — when found.'

'Hughes robbed him?' Markham

frowned. 'Took his money, just like that?'

'Maybe he was told to take it,' suggested Steve. 'As a reward for, say, contacting the King organisation before calling the local police. Maybe Shiel had something on him King wanted to remain private. I don't know. But I do know that Hughes was greedy. Maybe he held something back. He was called and a rendezvous arranged. He wrote down the address — I spotted the faint traces where his stylo had bitten through the paper. He kept the date. He was killed.'

'It makes sense,' admitted Markham. 'It could have happened as you say. King wouldn't have trouble finding an assassin to do the job.' He made an impatient gesture. 'But this is all surmise. There's no way of proving it.'

'I know that.'

'So it's a dead-end.'

'No,' said Steve. 'I don't think that it is. Hughes was a greedy man.' He explained. 'He wanted to milk the cow while he had the chance. He'd been paid off once and he wanted the same again. He figured that he'd get it too. What would give him that confidence?'

He saw the light begin to dawn in Markham's eyes.

'He had a copy of whatever it was he offered. Photostats maybe. That's why he was stripped, to make sure that nothing incriminating was found on the body. But Hughes might have wanted insurance.'

'Another copy,' said Markham.

'There was a self-service shop near the rendezvous,' said Steve. 'A kid who hangs around there remembered Hughes. He went into the shop. They have a copying machine. Hughes mailed something before going to meet his killer. You don't have to think too hard to guess what it was.'

'No,' said Markham. 'But are we any better off? We don't know where and to whom he mailed it.'

'We can find out. He didn't have that many friends. My guess is that he mailed it back to himself maybe via an accommodation address. I've got men working on it.' Steve looked at Markham. 'All right,' he said casually. 'Now suppose you tell me just what it is that you've got on Linda Sheldon?'

Markham hesitated.

'Come on,' snapped Steve. 'You talked about coincidence. What has that to do with Linda?'

'We've dug up some information on her financial background,' said Markham slowly. 'It doesn't add up.'

'I know that.'

'She had a call while you were away. The caller phoned blind. Who does that without reason?'

'Did they talk?'

'A little. They have used a prearranged code.'

'Anything else?' Steve felt the dryness of his mouth. Markham nodded.

'One other thing,' he said. 'It came from your office while you were away. I guess you know what it is.'

'I know.'

'It gives her a motive,' said Markham. 'The best.'

He was right, it did. King had stolen the McKee effect from a woman. Patricia McKee was Linda Sheldon's maternal aunt.

7

It was raining, a thin mist of drizzle scheduled each night from twelve to two — thirty minutes error allowed either side. Tonight it had been early.

'She's coming.' Markham wore a communicator, the microphone tight against his throat, the receiver hugging the bone behind one ear. 'She's just left the apartment.' He pressed a switch and spoke soundless orders. 'The boys'll go in as soon as she's left the building,' he said. 'If there's anything to find they'll find it.'

'Tell them to look in the desk,' said Steve flatly. He stood motionless as Markham relayed the order, his eyes on the main entrance to the building. She would use it — there was no reason why she shouldn't.

'There she is!' Markham didn't move as the slim figure swung into the street and began to walk towards the tube. He waited until she was halfway down the block before striding in pursuit. 'It's in the bag,' he said. 'I'll bet a month's pay that's how she's carrying it.'

Steve didn't answer. Linda was too fashionable to wear contrasting accessories yet she was carrying a too-large handbag of the wrong colour to go with her coat and shoes.

They followed her into the concourse of the underground tubeway, waited as she bought a ticket, joined the crocodile down the escalator. A man brushed past them and went on ahead. A couple followed by two women fanned out on the platform, moving with a vague, familiar purposefulness. Steve raised his eyebrows.

'This one isn't going to duck out,' said the chief grimly. 'I've got six of my best pinning her down. We're along just for the ride.'

It took them halfway across the city. She made no effort to avoid pursuit, not even looking back when she changed trains, and Steve wondered if she were either very clever or very stupid. He didn't think that she was stupid.

They reached the air terminal and Markham grunted as she entered an automat.

'This is the same trick that Ransom pulled,' he said. 'She'll take a tray, find a seat, go to the powder room and duck out from there.' He scowled as she rose and went towards the washroom. 'See what I mean?'

'A ringer?'

'I shouldn't think so — not this time. The rooms here have two entrances. My guess is that she'll leave by the other.' Markham listened to the tiny voice vibrating behind his ear. 'Just as I thought. Let's go!'

She was still carrying the handbag and still seemed unaware of her followers. Steve slowed as she entered the terminal and caught Markham by the arm.

'This is too open,' he said. 'She knows me and if she spots me we'll have been wasting our time.' He jerked his head towards a coffee bar. 'We'll wait in here.'

Markham nodded, letting Steve buy the coffee, shielding the motions of his lips as he relayed orders.

'She's killing time,' he said as Steve joined him with the coffee. 'Looking at magazines, checking flight times — ' He frowned. 'Now she's powdering her face.'

'Using the mirror to look behind her.' Steve tasted the coffee, added sugar, stirred. 'What now?'

'Some action. She's going over to the public lockers . . . opening one . . . standing before it . . . stepping back. She still has the handbag.'

'Or one exactly like it,' said Steve.

Markham nodded. 'A bust,' he said disgustedly. 'They had this all worked out. She delivers the goods to a locker. Someone has planted the payoff in advance in a duplicate bag. They wait until she's well away and then go to pick up the goods.'

'You could grab them when they do.'

'Sure, but what would we have? A creep who knows nothing. If we don't grab him he'll take a cab and 'forget' the package. If we pick up the cabbie we can't prove a thing. If we don't he picks up another fare and that fare leaves with the goods. Maybe he'll pass it on. Maybe he'll deliver it. These boys are smart.'

'Just careful,' said Steve. He leaned back, closing his eyes, conscious of the fatigue that dulled his thinking. It had been a slim hope that Linda would lead them to Ransom, an even slimmer one that she would be able to guide them to those who had engineered the crash. Now it seemed that hope had vanished. It was like all the other leads in the case. He jerked fully awake as he heard what the chief was saying.

'No. You can't do that.'

'Why not?' Markham's voice revealed his own fatigue and irritation. 'We've enough to pull her in and that's what I'm going to do. She has a workshop hidden in that desk. That's evidence enough to pull her in for questioning.' His lips made a thin, cruel line. 'I'm tired of running around in circles and getting nowhere. She's broken the law and I'm justified in pulling her in.'

'Is that an order?'

'I'd rather you didn't take it as one. But I don't want you to act without my say so.'

'All right,' snapped Markham. 'You're the boss. What are you going to do now?'

'Talk to her. Where is she?'

Markham scowled, gave an order, listened to the answer.

'Back at the automat.' He sounded vaguely surprised. 'Now what would she be doing back there?'

★ ★ ★

She was sitting in the centre of the eating space, a slim, forlorn and vulnerable figure. The massed bays of the automat dwarfed her with their mechanical coldness. Steve fed coins into a slot, drew up a cup of coffee, sat uninvited at her table. Their eyes met.

'Mr. Delmonte. How nice.'

'Steve,' he corrected mechanically. 'What are you doing out so late?'

'Minding my own business. And you?'

'Running the world.'

He tasted the coffee, pursed his lips, drank it. It didn't help. Irritably he rose, drew more coffee and halted before a drug-dispenser. A quarter emu bought a

98

treble shot of wakeydope. He swallowed it, washed down the taste, went to draw more coffee. He looked at Linda where she sat, outwardly calm and apparently totally disinterested in everything around her. She looked very lovely.

He remembered what an older man had told him during his early days in the service.

'You can never be sure,' he'd warned. 'They could have lovely faces and wonderful figures but the mind inside could be warped all to hell. Remember that when you feel yourself beginning to fall for one. Don't ever get fooled by the package. It's the contents which count.'

It had been good advice. It was still good advice. Which didn't make it any the easier to take.

'I couldn't sleep,' she said as he rejoined her. 'I thought that it would be better to take a walk than to lie staring at the ceiling. Satisfied?'

He stared at her without answering, trying to fit a criminal mask over her face and then, suddenly, was tired of the whole dirty game of cat-and-mouse.

'Give me your bag.' He reached for it a fraction too late. He gripped the leather, pulled, yielded as she held it fast.

'Let go!' She was white with anger. 'Let go or I'll scream.'

'You little fool!' He kept his voice low; to an outsider he was an attentive escort whispering compliments. 'What kind of a game do you think you're playing? You're as near as nothing to being taken in for questioning. Do you know what that means?'

'I can guess.' Her voice was cold. 'But don't you have to have something called evidence before you can do that?'

'The police, yes. Security, no. I can have you arrested on suspicion. Do you want me to prove it?'

She looked at him. She read the anger and irritation in his eyes, the bleak determination ridging his jaw. She swallowed, no longer sure of herself.

'You've been watched,' he said coldly. 'Your phone tapped, your apartment searched. You know what was found in the desk. Do you want to tell me about it?'

'Tell you?' The lift of her eyebrows matched the rise in her voice. 'Confess, you mean? To what?'

'Stop playing games!' This time when he reached for her bag he was faster than she was. He opened it, lips thinning he saw the currency inside. 'Is this the pay-off?'

'Give me that!' She snatched for the bag. 'What are you doing? Give it to me!'

'Not until you tell me how you got it.' He waited then shrugged. 'No? Well, there are other ways. Maybe you'll be able to fool the lie-test but we won't let it rest there. We'll use drugs, shock, deep-therapy. It won't be pleasant for you but we'll get the truth and, if we ruin your mind in the process, you'll only have yourself to blame. He pushed back his chair. 'Come on.'

'Where are you taking me?'

'To headquarters. Are you going to walk or do I have to carry you?'

She didn't alter expression but her fingers picked nervously at the edge of the table and he knew that he had shattered her calm. He wasn't proud of the

101

achievement. Backed by the full weight of authority it was a small thing to browbeat one lonely girl.

'What,' she said finally, 'do you want to know?'

'The money. Is it a payoff?'

'Yes.'

'You've been selling adapted krowns?'

'Yes.' She anticipated his next question. 'I don't know who buys them. I never see the man. I was propositioned over the phone. I refused. Then a man came to see me. It was dark, he was just a voice in the night. He offered me a lot of money. I needed it and I — well, I took it.' She looked at him, her eyes defiant. 'I needed the money,' she said again. 'I had to have it.'

It was no defence but it was human and probably true.

'So that's all you know? You've never seen who's behind this?'

'No. I've only heard a voice which was probably disguised.'

He nodded then stared at her with sudden suspicion.

'Why are you here? I mean, why did

you return to this automat?' The explanation struck him as he asked the question. 'This was the exchange point! You switched the bag holding the krowns to one holding the cash. You did it in one of the toilets. The business at the terminal was to throw any followers off-track. Whose idea was that?'

'His. He gave me instructions. We had a code and set routines.'

'And you came back because, in some way, you hoped to spot him,' said Steve. 'You were wasting your time.'

'I suppose so.' She tried to smile and couldn't make it. 'What happens now?'

'I'm thinking about it. He frowned, annoyed at his lack of decision. She sensed what he was thinking.

'You can't be sure that I'm telling the truth,' she said. 'I can't blame you for that. But if I can prove that, at least a part of what I said is true, would it make any difference?'

'What part?'

'The reason I wanted the money.' Her eyes were full of appeal.

'All right,' he said curtly. 'Prove it.'

They caught a helicab and flew for an hour, sitting silent as the lights of the city fell far behind. They landed before the blank wall of a private sanatorium. Linda was known. A tall, cadaverous man dressed in soft green greeted her as they entered the building. The name on his tunic was Emil Linguard. He looked curiously at Steve.

'Mr. Delmonte is a friend,' explained Linda. 'We flew out together. How is Mark?'

'About the same.' Linguard didn't shrug but his tone conveyed the gesture. 'I've warned you against too high hopes, Miss Sheldon. We are doing our best but miracles are beyond us.' He turned to Steve and held out his hand.

'Are you a friend of Mark's?'

'No,' said Linda quickly. 'Of mine. He doesn't know my brother.'

'That can be rectified,' said Steve. 'I'd like to meet him.'

Mark was lying in a private room, a mound beneath a sheet to which were attached various machines. The head was a bandaged ball, the hands shapeless blobs. What little could be seen of his face looked like seamed and seared steak. The eyes were closed, the sockets empty.

'My brother,' said Linda. She was bitter. 'Now you know why I have to have money.'

'An accident?'

'Yes. He was in a crash. He should have died but he didn't. Some would have called him lucky.' She swallowed, on the edge of tears, then her voice grew firm. 'His spine is shattered. He's paralysed from the neck down. He cannot hear. He is blind. Without those machines he would die. Sometimes I wish he would.'

'And at others?' Steve kept his voice low from instinct, not necessity.

'I pray for a miracle. Hospitalisation takes money. Regrafts even more and he is beyond that kind of help. He needs a new, prosthetic body if he is to ever really live again.'

Steve didn't comment. He had his own ideas as to the extent which a man could change his body to artificial parts and still regard himself as a man.

'Linguard has been honest with me,'

she said. 'He has suggested euthanasia but I won't hear of it. I made him admit that there is a slim chance and I insisted that he take it. It costs money — I promised to supply it. Now — '

'Now there will be no more money. Is that it?'

She didn't answer. Reaching out he took her by the shoulders and stared into her eyes. 'Listen,' he said thickly. 'I know what the temptation must be but don't yield to it. You won't be able to help your brother from the inside of a prison. Remember that.'

He released her and left the room. Linguard met him outside.

'A fine woman that,' he said, nodding towards where she stood beside her brother. 'As a doctor I've learned to assess the value placed on the helpless by those responsible for their welfare. It isn't very high. At times you get cynical and then someone like Miss Sheldon happens along and restores your faith in human nature.'

Steve made non-committal noises.

'You didn't know her brother, did you?'

Linguard remembered. 'No, you said you didn't. A fine young man. Reckless as they came but that was a part of his trade. In his business you have to be reckless.'

'What was that?'

'His trade?' Linguard raised his eyebrows. 'Didn't she tell you? He was a rocket-race pilot. One of the best.'

★　★　★

It was quiet in the helicab on the way back to the city. For a long time she didn't speak and then, as the flaring sign on the Palace grew close enough to read, he felt the impact of her eyes.

'What is going to happen to me?'

'If you've told me the whole truth — nothing.'

'Do you mean that?' She turned to look at him full-face. Her eyes were luminous in the subdued lighting.

'I mean it.' He looked at her shoulders — too slim for the weight she had forced them to bear.

'I don't understand. How — ?'

'How can I condone what you've

done?' He shrugged, a part of his mind cynically questioning if he would have done the same had she been older, less attractive.

'You've used your skill and knowledge to make some easy money,' he said harshly. 'Society wouldn't blame you for that. But you adapted krowns to cater to kinks. That is a criminal act and that makes you a criminal. But not as far as Security is concerned. We aren't interested.'

'Thank you,' she whispered. 'Thank you.'

'But understand this. The local police have you marked as a suspect. If you continue in the business they'll jump. If you've got the sense I think you have you won't run the risk. Believe me, you wouldn't know what hit you.'

She didn't answer and he looked at her with sudden doubt. She could have fooled him. She could have turned the weapons of her sex against him to dull his suspicions. She had cause to hate King — more now than ever for his money could have helped her brother. She could have made the krown Murray had worn. If she had then he was abetting a guilty participant to a triple killing.

Then he saw the shine of her eyes and, suddenly; she was against him, the softness of her in his arms, her tears wet on his cheek.

He had never been able to harden himself to the sight of tears.

8

Marcus Edward King was in conference. He held a glistening strip of metal in his hands, turning it so that the light shone from the surface in iridescent splendour, his eyes and face expressionless as he listened to a technician.

'We shall be able to hit full-scale production within ten days of your say-so, Mr. King. The new model can be automated within a week which allows three days for us to a synchronise the machines. In two weeks we can be ready to flood the market.'

King nodded and looked at his Head of Advertising.

'Everything is set to go, Mr. King. I've planned a ten-day saturation of all advertising media. Public figures and film and TV stars have been signed to wear the new model at all times. I'm allowing a three-day period to overcome consumer inertia and two days for the new fashion-trend to become established. In two weeks we'll be able to dispose of all the factory can make.'

King nodded again and looked at the third man seated at the table. Mowbray, Head of Finance, cleared his throat.

'The initial outlay will be tremendous, Mr. King. Full coverage demands millions in preliminary outlay. We've managed to secure options on most advertising media but, for worldwide coverage, we need to secure those outside of our immediate influence. The trouble is that, as soon as our intentions become apparent, the market will harden and prices rise.'

He flushed as King raised an eyebrow.

'I realise that I state the obvious. I also realise that we are operating through the medium of various supernumerary companies. However, I was referring to those channels of communication controlled by our . . . ' He coughed. 'By the Cartel.'

'You were going to say 'by our competitors',' said King. 'Must I remind you that we have no competitors? I control the world-patents on the McKee effect in all aspects of its application. The Cartel cannot compete.'

'No, of course not, Mr. King. But they will resist any effort on our part to expand into their sphere of influence.'

'You seem to be very concerned with the obvious,' said King dryly. 'You are not paid for that. You are paid to recognise obstacles and to find a way around, through or over them. I shouldn't have to remind you of that.'

'No, Mr. King.' Mowbray's face was ashen. He remembered what had happened to Fromarch.

'Well?'

'We could co-operate with the Cartel, sir. They would be willing to let us use their channels in return for a chance to share the new model.'

'And if not?'

'It would be war, sir.' Mowbray was positive. 'Our organisation and resources against theirs.'

'Agreed,' said King. 'Would we win?'

'That depends on the immediate return on sales of the new model. At the present suggested price the answer must verge on the negative. I realise that the price has been carefully chosen but the profit margin is too low.'

'Automation will take care of that,' said the technician. 'The manufacturing costs will fall as production increases. You've seen the graphs?'

'Naturally.' Mowbray was curt. 'However there is an average-cost figure which cannot be lowered. Based on that figure, coupled with retailers margin, distribution costs, packaging and deterioration the answer is still doubtful. Add the possibility of labour strife, blockage of raw material, increase in freight charges and minor sabotage and the answer is negative.'

'I see.' King ceased toying with the metal band. 'Your suggestions?'

'Restrict the market to our own sphere of influence. With cheaper advertising and lowered distribution costs things will be in our favour.'

'Or?'

'Raise the basic wholesale price. Add five per cent and things would be in our favour. Add ten and we would win.'

'That is your considered opinion?'

'Yes, Mr. King, sir. It is.'

'All right,' said Marcus. 'This is what you do. Prepare a summary of both additions. Run a test-campaign on the machines. Include every imaginable unfavourable circumstance and adjust until you find the optimum price which will achieve victory under any set of circumstances.'

'It will take time, Mr. King.'

'I'll give you time.' Marcus looked at the technician. 'You find ways of cutting manufacturing costs. I want the lowest figure for the highest output. If you need new equipment then include the cost in your calculations. You can lower the determined life of the product if you have to.'

'I've gone as low as I can, Mr. King.'

'Go lower.' He stared at the Head of Advertising. 'Recheck your schedule of costs. You can get a thousand girls for the price of one public figure. Tackle the fashion-trend from both sides. You should know what to do.'

'Yes, Mr. King.'

'Right. Now move! All of you! I want the new schedules on my desk within seven days!'

He scowled after them as they left. Little men with limited imaginations needing the whip to keep them up to scratch. He would give them the whip. If there was to be war then he intended to win it.

And, knowing the Cartel, there would be war.

'Daydreaming, Mr. King?' Fullen had entered the room with his soundless tread. He closed the door and looked curiously at the metal circlet. 'The new model?'

'Yes.' Marcus held it high, turning it so that the light flashed from the machined and polished surface. A diffraction grating had been scored into the metal and it shone with all the colours of the rainbow. 'Pretty isn't it?'

It was more than that. It was an ornament every woman would want to bind her hair — one that every man would need to enhance his status. The glitter spoke of wealth.

'A simple little thing.' Marcus dropped it to the desk where it lay like a coiled and sleeping serpent. Fullen didn't answer.

'Well?' Marcus stared up at the psychiatrist. His eyes glinted with mockery. 'Don't you agree?'

'Does it matter what I think?'

'No,' admitted Marcus. 'It doesn't.' He reached out and touched the krown. 'With this we come to basics. We've done away with free choice. This krown will receive only what we want it to receive. Naturally, the price will be low.'

Low enough so that everyone could afford the new model. It would be hailed as a major breakthrough in manufacturing techniques and advertising would be careful not to mention that it was a special krown.

One that would soothe and calm the wearer and give a state of continual euphoria. One that could receive signals sent on a special band. A circlet that would give sub-aural commands.

Which would make the whole world, if Marcus had his way, into a captive audience.

'You don't like it do you?' Marcus looked up at Fullen, one hand still touching the krown.

'No.'

'Could you tell me why?'

'I don't like the idea of people being captive to something beyond their control. I don't like men and women being regarded as cattle.'

'What else are they?' King rose to his feet, eyes reflecting his contempt. 'They are sheep. They deserve to be sheared.'

'Yes,' said Fullen. 'I expected you to say that.'

'And why not? I've sheared them all my life. Those at the top have always done so. That is why they are at the top.'

'And, of course, the public doesn't really know what is good for them.' Fullen spoke with a tired sarcasm. 'It takes men like you, Mr. King, to give them what they should have.'

'Yes,' said King. He ignored the irony. 'Without men like me they would still be living in caves and picking lice. Some men are born to rule.'

'By Divine Right?'

'You could put it like that,' said Marcus. It was an effort to remain calm but he could not afford the luxury of rage at Fullen's tone. 'Not all men are equal. Some are better fitted to rule than others. Do you deny that?'

'No.'

'Then, if you accept the existence of a Creator, who else determines which men should lead and which should follow? Thus, those who rule, do so by Divine Right. You agree?' Marcus shrugged as Fullen made no reply. 'You are too cautious to commit yourself. Such caution is a common trait of a weak character.'

'As you say, Mr. King.' Fullen's voice was casual, his eyes veiled. 'When are you going ahead with the new model?'

'As soon as certain details have been resolved.' Marcus slipped the krown into a pocket. He looked at Fullen and shook his head. 'I can't understand your hypocrisy, Fullen. Men have always been subjected to propaganda. They have always had the choice of ignoring it. The new model will alter that right of choice.

After all, they don't have wear it. No one will force them.'

No one had to. Marcus knew his public. They would willingly wear the yoke.

* * *

High in the building Ransom sat at his ease in a small but comfortable room. He was being watched. Five men kept him under constant surveillance. They were men trained to penetrate disguise, to recognise the walk and stance and posture of a man rather than purely physical characteristics. Ransom didn't know they were there. If he had he wouldn't have let it bother him.

He rose as Marcus entered the room.

'At last,' he said. 'I was beginning to think that you'd forgotten me.'

'Sit down.' Marcus dropped into a chair, gestured Ransom to his seat. 'Why are you annoyed? You had no objection when I sent for you and asked you to stay.'

'No,' admitted Ransom. 'I didn't mind

staying. It suited my purpose.'

'And now?'

'Now I'm tired of being cooped up in this fancy cell. How about getting down to business?'

He was curt but Marcus wasn't annoyed. He had known this man a long time. Once he had treated him as a son. It had been safe to do that for there was no blood-bond between them — no fear that the prince would aspire to the throne. But he had created another danger. An overwhelming pride. He had tried to break it — and had lost his son.

'All right,' said Marcus. 'We had our social chat when you arrived. What I have to say now couldn't have been said earlier.' Marcus paused and then, softly. 'How much is life worth, David?'

'That depends.' Ransom was surprised at the question. 'I've risked mine for a week's keep and taken it from those who valued it less. If you want a short answer I'd say that life is worth everything a man owns — without it he owns nothing.' His eyes narrowed in suspicion. 'Do you want me to turn assassin?'

'No. I have all those that I need.'

'Then — ?'

'Shiel is dead,' said Marcus. 'You remember Shiel?'

'Harry? Yes, I remember him.' Ransom's voice held a note of mockery. 'When you kicked me out I thought that he'd be riding high. You always did like him.'

'I trusted him. Now he's dead.'

'Assassinated?'

'The police say not,' said Marcus. 'But how can you be sure when there are so many ways to kill a man?'

'You can't.' Ransom spoke from knowledge. 'Was there any reason for him to be a target?'

'I don't know. There could have been. He was working for me on a special assignment. Someone may have got wind of it — I don't know who or how. Maybe his death was due to natural causes after all but I daren't take any chances. That's why I sent for you.'

'Why?'

'I want you to take over where Shiel left off.'

'No.' Ransom shook his head. 'I don't need the work. I get along all right.'

'You did,' corrected Marcus. 'Since you've been my guest there have been one or two changes. I don't think that you would find yourself as popular as you imagine.' Marcus relaxed in his chair. 'In fact, David, if you refuse me I don't think that you will be around much longer.'

'Are you threatening me, Marcus?'

'Of course not, David. Why should I threaten? It's just that — well, you know my ways.'

'Yes,' said Ransom. He looked down at his hands and wondered at his self-control. They rested limp and flaccid on his knees.

'You've been under psych-observation since you arrived,' said Marcus. 'The Mourne-Baylis system. My techicians confirm what I had hoped. You have apparently grown up. I'm glad that you have forgotten the past.'

'Not forgotten, Marcus.' Ransom breathed deeply, then smiled. 'You don't forget being turned from a prince into a pauper.

But I'm a realist. The past is dead.'

'Yes, David. Quite dead.'

'So you want me to carry on where Shiel left off,' said Ransom. 'Your technicians say that I can be trusted. But why me?'

'Isn't that obvious? We've been out of contact for five years. As far as anyone knows you have every reason to hate me and still do. From my point of view you would make a perfect replacement for Shiel.'

'And, if Harry was assassinated, they might not be so quick on the trigger with me,' said Ransom thoughtfully. 'They might even be inclined to make a deal. Have you considered that?'

'Naturally.'

'Does it bother you?'

'No,' Marcus was contemptuous. 'It could even be to our advantage.'

'My advantage,' said Ransom quietly. 'You seem to be taking a lot on trust. How can you be certain that I won't be tempted — and fall?'

'Because you're not a fool!' Marcus bared his teeth in a humourless smile.

'You'd never live long enough to enjoy selling me out. I'd put so high a price on your head that assassination would be inevitable. But there's another reason. It just wouldn't pay.'

He smiled as he saw the look in Ransom's eyes. The old, familiar, hungry glow. Greed was an emotion that Marcus could recognise and understand.

★   ★   ★

The house was a barred fortress set in a secluded part of the city. The door opened to a special code. The tall, masked figure within had an eidetic memory. He listened as the cloaked man rapped his identification number. Beneath his mask Ransom sweated with impatience.

'A moment, sir.' The doorman moved to a panel, spoke, returned. 'Room twenty-one, sir. You will pay now, if you please.'

Ransom paid.

'Your known, sir.' Ransom felt the cool touch of metal clamping about his skull. 'Your whip, sir.' The leather was warm to his hand. 'Thank you, sir.'

Ransom went down a corridor and up a flight of stairs. Locked doors marched past; thin sounds seeping past the closures. Odd sounds. Kink-sounds. They were to be expected — it was that kind of house.

The door of room twenty-one opened, closed behind him. A man stood inside, masked, armed with a whip. He felt the fear of anticipation.

Ransom shared it.

'You — ?' He snarled and flexed his arm. The lash snapped spitefully across the room. This time the masked figure felt terror and a desperate hate.

Ransom shared it.

He shared the rage as his lash cracked home, the pain, the fear and the futile struggle. He felt his own anger and contempt grow beneath the stimulus — to increase as it reflected itself back at him. He fought with the whip as his weapon and could sense the emotions of his opponent, the terror as he tore the lash from the other's hands, the screaming, shrieking agony as he beat and beat and beat at the quivering, helpless mass of tissue.

He was sweating when he finished, his body drenched in perspiration, his nerves flaming from the shared emotion. Not at full-strength, he was not masochistic, but enough to feel the bite of the lash, the pain and terror and desperation.

From the corner of the room, mewing with pain, his opponent stared up at him, his eyes frantic beneath the mask.

The plastic surrogate of Marcus Edward King.

9

Steve woke with a sour taste in his mouth and the feeling that he hadn't slept at all. The wakey dope he had swallowed was taking its toll. He had the choice between taking more, going back to sleep or trying to ride it out. The phone jarred the air before he could make up his mind.

'Delmonte?' The face belonged to Security. 'You'd better get over here fast.'

'Trouble?' Steve longed for coffee, hot sweet and strong. The man shrugged.

'Don't ask me. Just get over here.'

It was an order that had to be obeyed but first came a shower, coffee and pills to kill the need for sleep. Thirty minutes later he entered the building that housed the local Security office. Dale Markham rose from a seat. Steve blinked at him.

'What are you doing here?'

'I'd hoped that you could answer that,' said the chief. 'Didn't you leave word at the office?'

'No. I've just woken up.'

'You look it.' Markham was unsympathetic. 'I checked the locker,' he said. 'It was empty. Did you get anything from the woman?'

'She's clear.'

Markham looked dubious, he was not the man to trust a woman's word.

'We went to see her brother in a private sanatorium,' said Steve. 'I'm having a rundown made on him and on his doctor, a man named Linguard. Did you get anything new from the circus?'

'No.' Markham sounded disgusted. 'I've traced back the plane and it's clear all the way back to the factory; Klien won't break and his boys know nothing. Someone is doing a sweet cover-job. My guess is that Klien knows more than he says but I can't prove it.'

'And Ransom?'

'Still no sign. We'll keep trying though, there's not much else to do. But I'll tell you one thing, Steve. This case is a damn sight more complicated than I like'

* * *

Karl Shiller looked up from his desk as the two men entered the inner office. He was not alone. A nondescript man sat to one side, seeming to fade into the woodwork. Steve wasn't fooled. He had met men like Jones before.

'Sit down.' Karl Shiller, Head of Northwestern Terran Security, gestured towards chairs. 'As you're connected with the case,' he said to Markham, 'I've invited you to this conference. I don't believe in internecine warfare between different branches of the law-enforcement personnel. We are all working for the common good. Naturally anything you hear is to be treated with confidence.'

'I understand,' said Markham.

'Good.' Shiller looked at Steve. 'When you asked for a complete background check on Shiel I thought that you were shooting in the air. I rode along because it was your career that you were risking. What made you suspicious?'

'Something didn't make sense,' said Steve. 'Why should he be in Malibu? Why should he die? What was he doing?' Steve shrugged. 'Call it a hunch.'

'It paid off,' said Kari. 'Shiel dying the way he did was pure coincidence. Sometimes I think that police work would be impossible without it. All right, let's look at it. Shiel was found dead. He worked for King. The hotel detective, Hughes, thought that he would be smart. He phoned the King Organisation before he called the police. Shiel was carrying something King didn't want found. Hughes mailed it and took the money in the wallet as his payoff. So far, so good. But Hughes was greedy and tried to exert pressure. He copied whatever it was and asked for more. He met someone who killed him.'

'One of King's assassins?'

'Probably, Steve, it makes sense.' Karl looked at the agent. 'You were right about what Hughes must have done. We've found the copy. He'd mailed it to himself.'

'And?'

'We've deciphered it. It makes — interesting reading.' Shiller stared broodingly at the top of his desk. 'Shiel was an odd character,' he said. 'He was one of those men who have a love for paper and the written word. He kept notes.' He shrugged. 'More coincidence.'

'This case is lousy with them,' said Markham. 'There are so many that they cancel out.'

'Or make a peculiar kind of sense,' corrected Steve. 'How far have you got with the background check on Shiel?'

'Not too far but far enough,' said Shiller. 'Once we'd deciphered his notebook it was easy. Jones here,' be gestured towards the third man, 'dug up enough to make sense. It could also account for Ransom's disappearance. King must need a replacement for Shiel.'

'Not Ransom.' Markham was emphatic. 'He would be the last man King would pick.'

'Because they had a fight?' Shiller was cynical. 'Where money is concerned emotions take second place. King would use the man who suited him best. Ransom fits the pattern.'

'I don't see that,' protested the chief. 'Ransom hates King.'

'Maybe, but money soothes a lot of

wounds and King has money. But that isn't the only reason. The psych-boys have run behaviour patterns on what is known of King and Ransom. If you know enough about a man you can usually predict his reactions to any set of given circumstances. Ransom hates King, sure, but that is the very reason he would agree to replace Shiel. He has the strongest motive in the world to find what Shiel was looking for. King knows that. He also recognises the danger but, obviously, can guard against it.' Shiller rested the palms of his hands flat on the desk. 'So there it is. It fits and the probability of it being correct is nine point three — almost certainty.'

'Wait a minute,' said Markham. He was frowning. 'I don't get this. What was Shiel looking for that's so important?'

'Immortality,' said Shiller.

The word held such connotations that for a moment there was silence then Markham snorted his contempt.

'Crazy!'

Steve remained silent. He was thoughtful.

Shiller shook his head. 'No, whatever King is he isn't crazy. He knows what he's doing.' He looked at Jones. 'Tell them.'

'All right,' said the nondescript man. He took a sheaf of papers from an inside pocket. 'The transcript of Shiel's note-book,' he explained. 'Shiel knew him very well. King has a pathological fear of death. He isn't unique in that but he has the advantage of being so rich that he can do something about it. He realises that life is worth all he possesses. So, quite simply, he is trying to buy life.'

'Life, yes,' said Steve. 'He can buy regrafts and body-parts — but immortality?'

'He sees nothing futile in the quest,' said Jones. 'Maybe because he wants to believe in it so much. But for the past thirty years he has attacked the problem from three angles. The mechanical, the metaphysical and the actual. The mechanical means of extending life are too well known for me to go into detail. Artificial hearts, lungs, stomachs and the rest of it. Such means work but are limited. They also cripple the patient and make him totally dependent on others.'

'And King wouldn't like that,' said Steve.

Jones nodded. 'King's father died while attached to such a machine. The experience would not be conducive to trust. The metaphysical he has tackled by means of adapted krowns. The ideal is to effect a total change of personality. If successful it could mean that a man would live forever simply by switching from body to body. The snags are that the resident personality cannot be totally destroyed and, as far as we know, the invading personality cannot survive the death of its physical body.'

'Just as well,' said Markham grimly. 'When I kill a crook I like to know that he's dead.'

'And the actual?' Steve ignored the Chief's comment.

'Personal immortality,' said Jones. 'The method he likes best. The one for which he is prepared to spend his entire fortune.' He paused and gestured with his papers. 'The one Shiel was looking for when he died.'

And the one, thought Steve grimly, that Ransom, if Shiller was right, had been told to find.

What sort of man would trust an enemy with the secret of his immortality?

'I don't believe it,' said Markham. 'You can't just walk out and find a thing like that. It doesn't make sense.'

'It does if you know where and how to look,' said Jones. 'It does if you are desperate enough and rich enough to investigate every possibility. And it makes even more sense if you are convinced that what you are looking for actually exists.'

'But immortality?' Steve was doubtful.

'Let us call it extended life,' said Jones. 'Then, perhaps, you won't be so incredulous. And it is perfectly possible that such a thing does exist. People who have so long a lifespan that they are, to all appearances, immortal The legend of Cartaphilius is a case in point. There we — '

'The Wandering Jew!' Markham snorted his annoyance. 'Must we dabble in superstition?'

'There are many who would not call it

that.' Jones leaned forward a little, seeming to come at once alive and real. He was, Steve noticed, intensely serious. 'The legend is simple. A man was given a command that he would not die — and he did not die. I'm not arguing as to the truth of the legend. I'm merely saying that, in the light of present knowledge, such a psychic shock could have precisely that effect. What a man believes will, to that man, be true. We know the relationship between mental conviction and physical health. Psychosomatic medicine is very real.'

'Are you saying that King is looking for this man?' Markham was derisive. 'King — looking for the Wandering Jew?'

'Of course not.' Jones restrained his annoyance. 'I simply mentioned the legend as an example. There are others. Methuselah and his contemporaries who, if we are to believe in the old records, lived almost a thousand years. But that is beside the point. The main thing is that King has reason to believe that there are certain people among us who have lived incredibly long lives. When you come to think of it such people are more or less inevitable.'

'Freaks,' said Steve. 'Mutations.'

'Exactly. In an infinite universe anything can happen. The race is continually changing and we are subject to mutation at all times. Some mutations are harmful and short-lived. The successful ones we wouldn't know about. The ancients weren't so reticent. It isn't straining credulity too far to believe that, if Methuselah and his contemporaries were actual living people, their genes could carry the seeds of extended life. Such genes could, by chance, have combined in one person to give him that extended lifespan. Or there could be successful mutations with that characteristic.'

'Yes,' admitted Markham reluctantly. 'I suppose that could happen.'

'It has,' said Shiller. He nodded to Jones. 'Continue.'

'King told Shiel to discover any such persons. It was his special assignment. Shiel was a clever man and used his imagination. He checked Central Registry. He bought time at Cee West and asked the computer what he should look for. He went through a mountain of old files, medical records, rare blood groups. He investigated cases of freak accidents in which the person involved should have died but was unhurt. He searched insurance records and delved into case histories. He must have spent millions in cash and twenty years of time. He found what he was looking for.

'He found a man who has lived for a long, long time. The one man Shiel could discover who has what King would give his fortune to possess. The secret of longevity.'

'His name?' Markham leaned across the desk. He was interested, his previous incredulity forgotten in the new flush of conviction. 'What is his name?'

'That,' said Shiller dryly, 'is the one thing Shiel didn't write down.'

The room was a clutter of machines attended by busy operators. The air was permeated by a dull electronic humming. Shiller looked down at the activity from the balcony then turned to Markham.

'This is the heart of Security,' he said.

'The trick is to be at the right place at the right time and before any trouble has a chance to get beyond the hopeful stage. That's where we have the advantage over you police. You only come in when it's too late.'

'The difference between prevention and cure,' said Markham. He nodded towards the machines. 'What are they looking for?'

'Potential trouble. At the moment we're concentrating on King. We know about his new model krown and have a pretty good idea of what it can do. As yet making and selling it is perfectly legal.' Shiller looked up as an aide came towards him. 'Trouble,' he said. 'I'm wanted. Take over, Steve.'

'A nice guy,' said Markham as the Head of North-Western Security moved away. 'He doesn't automatically assume that a cop is too dumb to understand what is going on. I like that.'

'Shiller used to be a cop himself,' said Steve. 'Did you get what he was talking about?'

'I think so. King is up to something

that you people regard as potential trouble. From what I can make out there's nothing you can do about it. How do you handle things like that?'

'We have our ways.' Steve didn't explain that most of them were impromptu and many of them were illegal. They worked, that was all that counted. 'For example, we could persuade King's rivals to take action against him. Or we could bring an action in the courts on the grounds of misappropriation of basic patents, things like that. We could even ferment a strike at the factory.' He saw Markham's expression. 'It's a messy business but what choice do we have? The tycoons control politics. If we're to stop them slicing up society like a piece of cake we've got to fight them as we can.'

'Them?' Markham looked baffled. 'I thought that Security was concerned with external enemies. The Martian Combine, even the Luna Co-operative.'

'Our most dangerous enemies are those within our own society,' said Steve. 'Take King. If he makes his new krown he will trigger off a commercial war. That would mean real hardship for millions. The point isn't that he might win or lose but that we don't want a war of any kind. So we have to do our best to stop it.'

'How?' Markham looked at the machines below. 'I see. That's what they're looking for?'

'We're running test schedules based on assumed data. Will King start a war? How will he operate if he decides to flood the market with his new model? Will he risk upsetting the *status quo*?' Steve shrugged. 'As yet the answers are negative. He is too old to risk everything he owns and, as he has no children, he isn't interested in the prospects of founding a dynasty. King is basically a very selfish man. He has no intention of working so that someone else can enjoy the fruits of his labours.'

'So there will be no war.' Markham sounded satisfied. 'You're just — ' He broke off as he saw Steve's face. 'Have I missed something? The crash?'

'That's still a mystery,' admitted Steve. 'As far as we can discover the Cartel had nothing to do with it. And yet, whoever did it, had to have a reason. Maybe we've just found out what it was.'

'King's search for immortality?' Markham shook his head. 'I still think that's a pipe dream.'

'Maybe. But King believes in it and that's all that counts. If he is convinced that he is going to live forever — ' Steve shook his head. 'God help the world if he ever finds what he's looking for,' he said softly. And then, with sudden anger: 'Damn Shiel! Why didn't he write down the name?'

10

The name was Joe Langdy. Before that it could have been Joseph Marsh, Jymkin Wygate, Julius Aurelous — but now it was Joe Langdy and likely to stay that. Modern records insisted that a man be born and be able to prove it. Modern methods had made a number more important than a name; a row of figures which placed a man snugly in Central Registry and provided documents vital for welfare, taxation, employment, the paper-oil of a complex society.

Joe Langdy whose ex-wife worked as a chambermaid in the Hotel Excel.

She was nervous as she faced Ransom, her hands fretful, looking everywhere but into his eyes. He forced a comforting warmth into his voice.

'Please relax, Mrs. Langdy,' he urged. 'You don't have to be afraid of me. I'm not one of those government men always asking questions and making trouble. You can talk to me as you did to Mr. Shiel.' He recognised her blank expression. 'The man who died in room 2552,' he reminded. 'Did he talk to you?'

'No, sir.' Privately she wondered if Ransom was some kind of a kink. Her experience of the wealthy had done nothing to enhance her respect.

'Look,' said Ransom easily. 'I'll come straight to the point. I want some information and I'm willing to pay for it.'

'How much?'

'That depends.' At last he had aroused her interest. 'You won't regret it if you help me.'

'I want a thousand.' It was more than she needed but there was no sense in selling herself short. Ransom knew better than to appear too eager.

'As I said, that depends. Now, I want to know about Joe Langdy. Were you legally married?'

'Yes.'

'Any children?'

'No. Sam, my son, he was by someone else. Joe and me never had children. He treated Sam as if he was own boy though.'

'How long since you parted?'

'Close on twelve years. Joe left me. We were divorced almost ten years ago.'

'Why did he leave you?'

'I don't know.' She twisted the hem of her coverall, a pathetic figure who had long lost the urge to battle life and was content to accept what came without anger or question. 'I think that maybe he was just bored. He'd travelled a lot and was used to being on the move. I guess it was that.'

'Do you know where he is now?' It was a hopeless question but it had to be asked. Ransom wasn't disappointed at the answer. 'No? Well, did he keep in touch? A letter, postcard, airgram? Nothing on your birthday? Christmas? Anniversary?'

As if a man like Joe could remember all his anniversaries.

'No.' She shook her head. 'Wait. I think he sent Sam a card or two. They were close.'

'Sam? Your son? Where is he now?'

'Working on a sea-farm.' Mention of the place reminded her of Sam's need of cash. 'Are you going pay me, mister?'

Ransom pulled bills from his pocket, counted a thousand I.M.U's, held the remainder in his hand. 'Go on, pick it up. It's yours.' He watched her trembling hands scoop up the money. 'Now listen to me. I want you to tell me everything you remember about Joe. His likes, dislikes, hobbies, fancies. Where he'd worked and where he wanted to work. What he could do. Everything.'

She hesitated, biting her lip.

'Is he in trouble, mister?'

'No. I just want to find him. To give him some money that's due.' Ransom riffled the notes in his hand. 'I get paid for doing a quick job. Now, tell me about him. I'd like to know all about Sam as well.'

Again she hesitated. Slowly he counted out another thousand birds, hypnotising her with the sight of the cash.

'Talk and this is yours.'

She talked, and long before she had finished, he had decided that she had to die. There was nothing emotional about it. There was only the necessity of keeping a source of information private.

He did it with the prick of a pin.

She walked from the room, glowing with the confidence of wealth, not even annoyed at the clumsiness of the man who had been so curious. As he had passed over the money he had scratched her hand. It was a small scratch. A kitten would have given worse, but though she walked and smiled and breathed she was dead.

She would fall in three hours plus or minus ten minutes.

Long before that Ransom had checked out of the hotel and was on his way. A call to a firm of lawyers gave him an address. A call to the address told him nothing — it was an accommodation address used by transients. A dead end.

A call to the sea farm told him that Sam was still working out his contract. Joe and he had been close. It was possible that the boy knew more than his mother. Ransom picked up the phone, punched a number, replaced the receiver as he changed his mind. A charter plane would be fast but would leave a glaring trail. There were other, safer means of travel.

He took his time getting to the coast.

* * *

The agent was a shrivelled man with a thin mouth, skin scarred by broken capillaries and distrustful eyes. He stared at Ransom and sniffed.

'What you want to go down to the farm for?'

'It's Lobscombe's farm, isn't it?'

'Sure.'

'Then that's why I want to go down.'

The agent grunted and scratched his chin. The fingers lifted to his hair. Both needed a wash.

'You a kink?' he said abruptly. Ransom hesitated. 'I knew it,' crowed the agent. 'I can smell 'em a mile. You wanna go down to the fifty-fathom line and see how they do it. Right?'

'Wrong.' Ransom lifted a finger to his forehead. 'Feel how they do it. Get me?'

'I get you.' The agent looked down at his grimed hands. 'They lose a lot of men down at Lobscombe. It's a tough life below the fiftyline. They live hard and play the same. What's on your mind?'

'Kicks. Enough?'

The agent shrugged.

'Get me to the farm,' said Ransom. 'Give the supervisor the word. A hundred birds for you and the same for him. Four hundred more for each of you when I get out.'

'When will that be?'

'An hour. A day. A week. What does it matter?'

'When do we collect?' The agent didn't look at Ransom. He seemed fascinated by his broken nails.

'I'll deposit the cash at the bank. They pay you when I thumb the order — in person. If I have an accident you get zero. Is it a deal?'

'Well — ' The agent hesitated. 'I'll be taking a risk. It's all right for Bronson, he's the super, but he's got an out. I'm responsible for sending you down. If anything should happen — '

'You'd wake up dead,' snarled Ransom. He towered over the agent, eyes cold, mouth cruel. 'Play along and you get plenty. Cross me and you get what's coming. I'm not alone in this.'

The agent shivered. Ransom relaxed, not wanting to frighten the man off.

'Listen,' he urged. 'What's it to you? You send me down and give the super the word. When I want out he checks me unfit. Claustrophobia, maybe, or pressure sickness. Hell, you must get it all the time.'

'I do,' said the agent dryly. 'But they stay down regardless. Lobscombe's a tough farm, mister.' He shrugged. 'All right. You've got yourself a deal. Let's go.'

Ransom went down with a party of five. A handful of miserable end-of-the-roaders who had signed up in desperation and who now wished they hadn't. The sub-pilot was jocular and had a warped sense of humour.

'Thirty fathoms,' he announced. 'A hundred and eighty feet of water. Not much but enough to give you a real, loving squeeze.'

And later.

'Close to the fiftyline. One mistake this deep and you're dead. If we split our seams now we'd be pasted over the inside of the hull, but don't worry about that. Don't worry when you bleed at the nose either — it's when you bleed at the eyes that it's serious.'

And finally.

'Here we are, folks. Lobscombe sea farm. One of the best installations of its kind on the ocean floor. Home sweet home, Constant running water, free medical attention and if you die, it won't cost a thing.' He laughed at his own humour. He was the only one.

* * *

Bronson met them as they passed through the airlock. The supervisor was a swarthy man with a barrel chest and the bowed legs of a jockey. He jerked a thumb down the corridor.

'Get in room fifteen and sort yourselves out. Report at number three airlock in fifteen minutes.' He stared at Ransom, noting his clothes, his posture. 'You the visitor?'

'That's right.'

'Follow me.'

He led the way down a narrow corridor reeking of damp and heavy with the smell of rotting seaweed. A door opened into a spacious cubicle. The walls were covered with coloured prints of naked women. A bunk stood in one corner, a bottle and glasses on a table. Like its occupant, the room was soiled, bleak and dirty.

'Fred passed the word,' said Bronson after he had kicked shut the door. 'Want a drink?'

'Thanks.'

Bronson rinsed the glasses at a faucet, filled them from the bottle, downed it with a single gulp. Ransom sipped, raised his eyebrows, sipped again. It was good liquor.

'Another?' The supervisor tilted the bottle. 'What's my cut out of this? I want to know.'

'Five hundred.'

'For what?'

'You've got a man down here. I want to see him. Name of Prince, Sam Prince.' Prince had been Ellen's name before she married Joe. 'You know him?'

'That creep? Sure I do.' Bronson emptied his glass

'Always bitching about conditions and trying to dodge work by reporting sick. Sick! I'll give him something to be sick about if he doesn't watch it.'

'Where is he now?'

'Where would you think? In the infirmary. You know, guys like that make me sick. They take the job and then never stop whining about it. From what I hear he wants to buy himself out.' He looked accusingly at Ransom. 'Is that what you want? To buy him out?'

Ransom shook his head.

'It's none of my business if you want to waste the cash,' said the supervisor. 'Maybe it would be better at that if you did. Let him carry on the way he had and something will happen to him.'

'Like that, is it?'

'You know how it is. Down here a guy has to play along. If he doesn't then accidents can happen. Too bad but that's the way it is. The fiftyline can be dangerous.' He winked and hefted the bottle. 'Want another?'

'Let me buy this one.' Ransom tossed a fifty-bird note on the table. 'When can I see him?'

'Prince?' The supervisor squinted at a wall-clock. 'Give it an hour. I've got to break the new men in and see the new shift out. After that I'll take you down.' He waved a hand in a vague gesture. 'He'll keep. Now how about another drink?'

The infirmary held six beds two of which were occupied. One held the prone figure of a man. His breath rasped in liquid gurgles from his chest. Sam was in the other.

He looked at Ransom with the eyes of a tormented animal. His face and hands were thin, the skin a ghastly white. The mound of his body beneath the covers looked as if it belonged to a boy rather than a grown man. He tensed as Ransom sat beside him.

'I understand that you're in a little trouble,' said Ransom easily. 'Is that right?'

'Who are you? What do you want?'

'A friend. I want to help you. Your mother told me how to find you.'

'You've come to buy me out?' Hope blossomed in the sunken eyes. 'She sent you with the money?'

Ransom didn't answer.

'Mister,' said Sam brokenly. 'If you buy me out there's nothing that I wouldn't do. Nothing.'

'Tough, eh?'

'You don't know the half of it. It's like a jungle. They're all against me because I won't join in the gambling. Bronson gets a cut, did you know that? If you won't play he bears down on you all the time. Gives you the rough jobs, you know. If you give in and lose then you're here for life. Mister, I've got to get away.'

'Take it easy.' Ransom smiled down at the terrified man. 'I told you that I'm here to help you. You've got nothing to worry about. All I want is a little information.'

It took over an hour to get it.

They had been close, Sam admitted that. Joe had taken to him as if he'd been his own son and, after he'd gone, he'd kept in touch.

'Just a card now and again,' said Sam. 'You know the kind of thing. A place, a few words, things like that. He was in Arizona, then in China, he travelled a lot.'

He was wistful as he said it but Ransom had no time for nostalgia.

'The last time I heard from him?' Sam didn't have to remember very hard. 'That was just a short while back. He sent me a card.' He fumbled beneath his pillow. 'I kept it. He was always pretty good to me and I figured that, if I ever get out of here, I'd join up with him.' He held out the card. 'Here it is.'

Ransom took it. It was a thin, cheap communication slip. The date was recent, the franking stamp clear, the message brief.

'You should be here with me!'

The view on the front was one he had seen before.

'I'd like to keep this,' said Ransom. 'May I?'

'Well — ' Sam was reluctant to let it go. 'It's the only one I've got.'

'You can get others,' said Ransom. He rose and slipped it into his pocket. 'You can even send some yourself soon.'

Sam caught the implication.

'You mean that you're going to get me out of here?'

'Sure.' Ransom stepped forward. He jerked the pillow from beneath Sam's head and dropped it over his face. His arms tensed as he held it in position. 'Sure,' he whispered. 'I'll get you out of here.'

★   ★   ★

The music was Sorgach's Conquest of Space. It flowed from the tri-speakers, filling the apartment with frenetic melody, building a constricted world of steel, plastic and alloy, turning the comfortable room into a narrow coffin rank with the sweat of fear, reminiscing with the pulsing notes of a dirge before flowering into a soaring paean.

Linda Sheldon listened to it as she had a thousand times before. The ending didn't suit her mood. Adjusting the controls she returned the recording to the point where the slow roll of drums merged with the insidious tapping of the tympani, the beat of the percussions slowed to a rhythm below the normal beating of the heart, monotonous in its saddening repetition.

A dirge for those who had died.

A dirge for a dead brother.

Steve rose and crossed the room. He turned a switch and the music died. He caught her hand as she reached forward.

'No,' he said firmly. 'Let the dead bury the dead.'

'Are you quoting at me?'

'Just repeating some excellent advice. Here is some more. Sufficient unto the day is the evil thereof.'

'From the Bible?'

'Yes. Mark is dead. Tearing yourself apart with grief won't help either him or yourself.'

'He was my brother,' she said dully. 'While he was alive I had something — some family. Now he's gone.'

'Isn't it better this way?' He held her by the shoulders, very conscious of the slim loveliness of her between his hands. 'Face up to it, Linda, Are you sorry for him or for yourself?'

'I don't understand.'

'I think that you do. Mark wasn't very close to you at the best of times. He was too independent for that. Then he had his accident and, suddenly you found yourself all-important to him. Now he's dead and that need no longer exists. Is that why you mourn?'

'You're horrible!'

'I'm realistic. It's my job. But what are you asking? Did you really want your brother to drag out his life as a hopeless cripple? Did you hate him so much that you grieve because he has escaped such a fate?'

He released her and adjusted the machine. He switched on and the soaring paean filled the apartment, the accelerated tempo designed to induce euphoria. He waited until it was over, the abrupt ending shocking with its silence.

'Tell me about it.'

'What is there to tell?' She sat down, looking not at him but at her hands. 'Doctor Linguard called. He said that Mark was dead. Natural causes.' She looked at him, helplessly, eyes brimming with tears. 'That's all.'

Steve didn't speak. He didn't tell her that the call had been monitored, the death investigated. He had simply paid a social visit at a time when he hoped his company would be appreciated.

'I'm sorry.' She took his hand and held it in her own. 'I'm afraid that I'm not very good company. Please forgive me.'

'Of course.' He returned the pressure of her hand. 'Would you like to go out somewhere? To eat?'

'No thank you.'

'A show? A tri-di?'

'No.' She managed to smile. 'I don't feel very much like entertainment. Why don't we just — ' She broke off as the drone of the attention signal came from the phone. 'Excuse me.'

She rose and answered the instrument then looked at Steve.

'It's for you.'

Shiller's face looked from the screen. It was grim, his eyes bleak.

'Steve! The case is breaking. Ransom's been spotted.'

'Good. Where?'

'In the city. Ellen Langdy is dead.'

'Ransom?'

'He was there. She died of one of those gimmick poisons and we could never prove that he did it but I've no personal doubt. My guess is that he killed her to shut her mouth.'

'Then she must have known something about the man Shiel was looking for. His name, perhaps. Ransom must know who and where he is.'

'That's what I figured.'

'Then bring him in for questioning. Damn it, Karl, why the delay? This thing is too big for us to be squeamish. Bring him in and tear him apart. Let's get at the truth before it's too late.' He saw Shiller's expression. 'What's wrong?'

'We're already too late, Steve. Ransom was spotted at the spaceport. He's gone to the moon.'

'Luna?' Steve felt the sudden constriction of his stomach. 'He's got away?'

'Yes, Steve,' said Shiller grimly. 'He's gone to Luna — where we have no jurisdiction at all.'

11

On the moon men were goldfish living in tight little aquaria of light, heat and air gouged deep in the rocky crust. Two generations had given them their own standards of beauty, art and ethics. They had a workable society

'A peach,' whispered the girl invitingly. She was tall, slim to the point of freakishness, with a heart-shaped face and elfin eyes. 'A whole peach soaked in brandy, golden with the kiss of the sun — yours for fifty birds.'

Ransom ignored the seductive voice.

'A breast of chicken, milk-fed on open range, seeped in wine and served with jelly. Ecstasy for one hundred.'

The lilting voice became a little petulant.

'A little high? How high is too high? For five I can supply an apple, for seven a wedge of cheese, for ten a handful of dried grapes. Or perhaps I aim too low?

For two hundred a bowl of caviar, black as space, each egg an ebon gem. A stronger taste? Real venison, rich with flavour, succulent with natural juice. Meat fit for a king.'

'King has meat,' said Ransom and laughed at his own play on words. He felt a little drunk and more than a little light-headed. His earth-accustomed heart was pumping vast quantities of blood through his brain. He felt exhilarated.

'King has all the meat he can eat,' he said. 'Get it?'

'A joke, sir?'

'A damn good joke.'

'Then I join you in laughter.'

Ransom nodded and laughed then sobered. Sourly he looked at the plastifilm walls, the severe lighting. The tables and chairs were of crushed and bonded stone. One end of the room had been planed flat, the surface glowing with the pulsing notes of a colour-organ. A tinkling fountain provided one of the most welcome sounds on the moon — the most dreaded was the hiss of escaping air.

'Join me in a drink,' he invited.

Reaching forward he hefted the bottle. 'A rare vintage,' he mocked. 'Tanged with the flavour of urine, pervaded with the stink of yeast, brewed beneath an artificial sun. A fit beverage for tramps, touts and tourists.'

'You mock, sir?'

'Why not? I'm a tourist. You're a tout. I'm looking for a tramp.'

He sipped his drink, noting her silence, instinct pricking him with warning. He had been cautioned against the euphoria of low-gravity and had been given pills to take in case of need. They were small, dark, easy to swallow, hard to hold. One slipped and rolled on the floor.

'Allow me, sir.' The girl stooped and offered something in her open palm. Ransom slapped it away.

'Grow up,' he sneered. 'I was pulling that one when I was twelve.'

'You wrong me, sir.'

'Then you're a fool. Never miss an opportunity. Doping a drunk is nothing spectacular but it's better than starving.'

He sat and waited for his heart to cease its insane pounding. Beside him the girl whimpered as she nursed her wrist. It was painfully thin, easily injured. Moon-born she lacked the robust strength of those reared on Earth.

The noise offended him. He rose and looked down at the elfin face.

'Here.' He threw a five-hundred note before her. 'Buy yourself some salve.'

Outside he wandered the underground hive that was Tycho. He found the commercial section and halted before a door. The Condor Employment Agency was open for business. He went inside.

The place was barely larger than his hotel room. A counter cut it into two sections. On his side some posters advertised the advantages of the culture complex at Clavius; a cheap round trip to Schickard, the benefits offered by the Martian Combine and the programme of the local tri-di. There were no seats and no customers.

The far side was fitted with office furniture and a faded blonde. She smiled at Ransom, pricing his clothes with a glance.

'Sir?'

'I want a job.'

'A job?' He sensed the subtle change in her attitude.

'Name? Profession?'

'Weston. I've done most things. Repair work, copter pilot, some building construction. I'm good with my hands.'

'Can you be more specific?'

'Rock miner.' Someone had to gouge out the living space. She wasn't impressed.

'Your papers?'

'I haven't got any.' He read her eyes. 'I lost them. I had a few drinks too many and, when I woke, they were gone. Are they important?'

'We have to have them. Address?'

'No address either.' He lowered his voice. 'I only arrived a while ago. On the Kingflash. Look, I'd like to get fixed up with papers and a job. If you could fix it for me I'd be willing to pay. Those crooks who stole my papers didn't get — ' He broke off, looking over her shoulder towards the open door at the rear, at the man who came towards them.

'A little trouble, Miss Fisher?'

'No, Mr. Condor. It's just that this man

166

has no papers and no address.'

'I see.' Condor lifted the flap of the counter. 'I think that we had better continue this in my office. This way, Mr. Weston.'

The rear office was a reflection of the personality of the owner. It was painfully neat and bare to the point of sterility. A colour tri-print of a city as seen from the air stood on the desk. It was the only ornamentation. Condor sat down, gestured to a chair, thumbed the pages of a folder.

'The Kingflash, Mr. Weston?' Condor pursed his lips as he looked at the folder. 'Surely there must be some mistake? No arrival of your name is listed for the Kingflash. Some other ship, perhaps?'

'Does every employment agency keep a record of all new arrivals?'

'If they are interested, as I am, and as the government agencies are. We have a government on the moon, Mr. Weston.'

'So?'

'A surprising number of people think that we haven't. They regard us as a collection of free-enterprise entrepreneurs but that isn't strictly the case. We have to have some system in order to survive. Men cannot live without air, Mr. Weston.'

'Ransom.'

'I beg your pardon?'

'My name isn't Weston, it's Ransom.' He produced his papers and threw them on the desk. 'I was testing a theory. Maybe you could tell me if it would work. I wanted to find out if it were possible for a man to arrive on the moon, change his name, take up regular employment. In other words, vanish. Could he?'

'Officially no. Theoretically it could be done but it would require collusion with another. Two men arrive. They exchange papers and one goes back as the other. Your man stays here under a different name. There are, of course, difficulties, but it could be done.'

'And without help?'

'Impossible.' Condor was definite. 'Before you can be employed you must obtain a resident's certificate. You can obtain one at the landing stage or at the Central Agency. All you have to do is to surrender your passport and declare your intention to stay.'

Ransom nodded. It was as he had hoped. A paper-trail could be followed and there was no real reason for Langdy to have changed his name.

'And if I had been robbed?'

'You could still obtain a certificate or a replacement,' said Condor patiently. 'You would know who you are and could prove it. Your arrival, for example, would be recorded.' He coughed. 'Is that all, Mr. Ransom?'

* * *

Central Agency was at the hub of Tycho. He crossed to a counter marked Information, spoke to a girl, waited as she checked a file.

'What is the reason for your request, Mr. Ransom?'

'A matter of inheritance.' He anticipated the expected question. 'I must get his personal signature and witness the signing.'

'I understand. Resident Records should be able to help you. Room 276 — follow the red line.'

It led to an anteroom filled with chairs, half-filled with people. Patiently Ransom waited his turn.

'Langdy? Joe Langdy?' The man behind the counter was old, tired, grotesquely fat. 'What do you want to know for?'

Ransom repeated his explanation.

'Have you a court order authorising the search?'

'Do I need one?'

'It's usual,' said the clerk. 'Our residents are entitled to privacy. We don't want them badgered by a lot of people from Earth.' His chuckle was a painful wheeze. 'Most of them come here for that very reason.'

'I'll bet,' said Ransom. He knew the type. A show-off know-all doing a routine job and making the most of it. Rub him the wrong way and he'd turn stubborn. 'I guess you know them all.'

'I can tell,' wheezed the clerk. 'Wife-leavers, debt-dodgers, some wanted for questioning, others one jump ahead of the law. When I was working at the landing stage I could pick them out in the first two minutes. Not that it mattered.

They'd come to us and old Mother moon took them in and made them her own. That's why they've got to be protected. Understand?'

Ransom smiled at the clerk. He knew the system. Labour was needed on the moon and the entrepreneurs didn't care too greatly where it came from. Luna had its sovereignty. If a man could get past the check-points on earth he was safe — and the moon gained a labour unit without the necessity of having to feed, clothe and educate him for the first, unproductive sixteen years of his life.

'So we've got to be careful,' wheezed the clerk. 'If we upset them too much they're liable to move on to Mars. Now, this Langdy, when did he arrive?'

'I don't know. Sometime in the past twelve years.'

'That long? What does he do?'

'I don't know what he's doing now. He used to be a male nurse.' He had been told that when Ellen had met him. He might still be doing the same thing. The clerk looked doubtful.

'Not much call for them here. The girls

take care of pat stuff. Anything else?'

'Nothing for sure.'

'That's too bad.' The clerk jerked a thumb behind him, where filing cabinets stood in ranked array. 'That's a lot of paper to go through, friend. I've a name and nothing else. First I've got to track down the name, get his number, check with permits, check with employment, medical, law and emigration. It'll take time.'

'How much time?'

'That depends. We're kept pretty busy. Say a couple of weeks.'

'Say a day,' suggested Ransom. He took a bill from his wallet and wrote on it. 'I'm sure a man like you knows how to cut corners. I'm staying at the Grand Luna. I've jotted down my room number. Call me when you get anything.' He handed over the bill. The clerk opened his eyes at the amount.

'All right, Mr. Ransom.' He was suddenly very polite. 'I'll do what I can, sir. Leave it to me.'

Back in the main concourse of Luna City Ransom hesitated, wondering if there was something more he could do. He decided against it. To rush around in a frenzy of unco-ordinated effort was to waste time, money and energy. The money didn't matter, King was paying, but such activity could arouse unwanted interest in both himself and the object of his search. He had put wheels in motion and now could only wait for something to develop.

He had a couple of drinks at a club, saw an indifferent tri-di, unusual only because it was uncensored, ignored a tout from the Martian Combine and finally went back to his hotel.

The Grand Luna was the last word in moonside luxury. The rooms were large with facsimile windows backed by living murals of earthside scenes. The air was scented with pine, rose or sea-spray. The faucets were unmetered. Each room contained a shower. There was a swimming pool for the use of residents. The dining room served fabulous food. The cost was astronomical.

Ransom took a shower, lingering beneath the needle-spray, careless of the fact that he was doubling his basic room-charge.

Then he went to bed.

He woke to the muted purr of the phone. The operator, hand-picked for beauty, trained in voice-modulation, smiled at him from the screen.

'A call for you, Mr. Ransom.'

'Put it through.'

'Yes, sir . . . ' Her features dissolved to be replaced by the obese visage of the clerk at Records.

'Mr. Ransom. Sorry if I woke you but you said it was urgent and — '

'What is it?' Ransom swung himself off the bed.

'I dug something up, sir. You talking about — you know who — being a male nurse put me onto it. I took a chance and it paid off. At least I think it did.'

'Yes?'

'A man named Langdy worked at Collinson's Health Centre. It's over in Maginus. I thought that you'd like to know, Mr. Ransom.'

'You thought right.'

'I'll keep at it but this might turn out to

be a shortcut. Shall I call if anything else turns up?'

'Yes.' Ransom stared at the fat, eager-to-please face. 'Keep working on it and contact me if you find anything new. You won't regret it.'

He cut the connection, waited, flashed the desk. The incredible beauty of the receptionist stared inquiringly from the screen.

'Sir?'

'Ransom here. I want to get to Maginus. Can you arrange it?'

'Certainly sir. If you will give me a moment?' It took a little longer. 'There is a scheduled ground-trip which leaves in eight hours time,' she said, looking at something beyond range of the scanners. 'Passengers to take own food and water. There is a first-class runner in twelve. Fare includes rations.'

'No aerial flight?'

'A short-shot rocket makes the circuit of Maurolycas, Maginus, Clavius, Longomontanus and back to Tycho every three days. Alternate routes each trip.' She smiled from the screen. 'The next flight is not for two days.'

'Damn. Is there any other way?'

'Only by private charter, sir.'

'Then fix it,' snapped Ransom. 'I want to leave in an hour.'

12

Next to Tycho Maginus was a village. A cluster of plastic bubbles clung to the ring-wall of the crater. A leveled space served as a landing field. A gap in the jagged heights had been cleared for ground transport. A lone beacon notified the universe that here, among the scree and stone, rested a habitude of Man.

'Collinson's Health Centre?' The recorder looked up from his papers and stared curiously at Ransom. 'Sure I know it. Decant five, sector eight, anyone will show you the way. Staying long?'

'Just a flying visit.'

'No air tax for one-day visitors. Reciprocal agreement. Your plane waiting?'

'Yes.'

'O.K. I'll take care of the pilot. Call me when you're ready to leave.' The recorder rubber-stamped Ransom's tourist travel book. 'Welcome to Maginus, Mr. Ransom.'

Collinson's Health Centre was a door

set in solid stone with an unobtrusive plaque bearing a cadecus superimposed over the name. It swung open and eyes peered at Ransom through the Judas window.

'Collinson?'

'Who wants him?'

'A customer. Go get him.'

The window slammed, time passed, the door opened. A man stood looking up at Ransom. He was a little over five feet tall. One shoulder was higher than the other. The spine appeared to be twisted and the back was humped. He had the classical features of a Greek God.

'I am Collinson,' he announced. 'And you?'

Ransom introduced himself.

'I see,' mused the hunchbank. 'So you lied to my doorman. He told me that you were a customer. Now it seems you just want to talk to me. You've come all the way from Earth just for that. I should be flattered.' His eyes brooded at Ransom. 'Did your parents love you?'

Ransom hid his surprise at the question. 'No.'

'Then you were fortunate,' said Collinson softly. 'My parents loved me. I was born here and they took me to Earth when I was very young. They wanted me to grow tall and strong. You see how they succeeded.'

'The gravity?'

'That, and other things. A helicab crash among them.' The hunchback shrugged. 'I tell you this so as to put you at your ease. Men of Earth do not like to see such as I.' He stepped back from the door. 'Enter.'

Behind the door were rooms filled with patients. By Earth standards Collinson was a freak but he was beautiful compared to those in his care.

'Extreme glandular hypertrophy,' he murmured as they passed mounds of fat and tissue lying slug-like on pneumatic mattresses. 'Very sad.'

They entered another room.

'Tropical disease, muscular atrophication, cardiac disorders. Incurable but we do what we can.'

'Naturally,' said Ransom dryly as he followed the cripple into his office. The

179

racket was plain. The low Luna gravity enabled the patients to live where, on Earth, they would have died. Collinson looked after them. They or their relatives paid him for his care.

'Langdy,' he said after Ransom had asked his question. 'Langdy? Langdy?'

'Joe Langdy. He worked for you as a male nurse.'

'Ah, now I remember.' Collinson's smile was a sneer. 'Yes, I did have him with me for a while.'

'He isn't here now?'

'No.' Collinson lifted his deformed shoulders. 'He and I had a difference of opinion and I had to let him go.'

'Why? Did you quarrel?' Ransom wasn't interested but he wanted information.

'Did I say we had quarrelled?' Again the sneer, the repulsive shrug. 'I, as you see, am not as fortunate as most men. Perhaps that is why I have so close an affinity with the afflicted. I understand them. I realise their wants and needs. I know how they wish to be treated. Langdy could not agree with me.'

'So you fired him. Where did he go?'

'He called me inhumane,' said the hunchback. 'He failed to realise that his way was the wrong way. The afflicted need no pity. They have their own strength.'

'Where did he go?'

'He didn't understand.' The dark eyes held a malicious amusement. 'He didn't understand the needs of those he secretly despised.'

'No? Well, Collinson, I do.' Ransom reached out and gripped a shoulder, the fingers grinding with trained skill against nerve and sinew. 'You're crippled and you hate those who are not. You get your revenge in little, spiteful ways and think you're smart. Well, don't play those games with me.' His fingers dug deeper. 'Answer and tell the truth or I'll come back and break a few bones. Where did Langdy go?'

'To the vats,' snarled Collinson. 'To the filth where you both belong!'

★　★　★

He meant the reclamation plant. Like agricultural workers on Earth the reclamation workers on Luna were at the bottom of the social heap. It was probably due to the notion that those who worked with dirt must, themselves, be dirty.

On the moon the dirt was sewage.

'Langdy?' The foreman wiped his hands on the seat of his coveralls then noticed Ransom's expression. 'Come into the shack. I've something there that will kill the smell.'

The shack was a small room adjoining the process vats. The something was one hundred and eighty proof alcohol.

'You get so that you don't mind it after a while,' said the foreman. 'Sometimes you get so that you hate to leave it. Of course, that takes a little time.'

He was talking of the work, not the liquor.

'There's a sort of seasonal rhythm to it,' he continued. 'You spread and process and wait for the sun to ferment the mash. You collect the gases, the vapour, the steam. Then, when the night comes, you open your sacs and let the stuff freeze. It dries right out and crumbles to a powder ready for use.' He helped himself to another shot of the alcohol. 'Like they say,' he ended with quiet pride. 'We use it all but the smell.'

'It must be a satisfying job,' said Ransom. 'Langdy?'

'I had high hopes of Joe,' said the foreman. 'I thought that maybe he was a natural. You know how it is, no one wants the job and we always need labour. But once in a while someone comes along just made for the work. I figured Joe that way. He had a feel for the job. He'd know when a batch was rich and when it was poor. He could tell to the minute when we'd got all we was going to get. Have another drink.'

Ransom had another drink.

'You don't get many like Joe,' sighed the foreman. 'He wasn't like the impressed men we usually get. I guess after working in that freak-factory this was a ball.' He stared at Ransom. 'Can you understand any man working in a place like that? No wonder Joe quit.'

'Where did he go?'

'Calvius, I think. Or was it Longo-monatus?' He yelled to a dingy figure tending one of the vats. 'Hey, Charlie! Remember Joe Langdy? Where did he go from here? Was it Calvius or Longomonatus?'

'It was neither. It was Maurolycus.'

Ransom went there. Another village. Another man who scratched his head and said, yes, he remembered Joe. A fine miner. A pity he'd moved on. To where? To Piccolimini, or was it Petavius? He wasn't sure.

Ransom tossed a coin, went to the wrong place, tried again and lost the trail. He paid off the charter plane and travelled as Joe would have done. He took scheduled transports crawling between the minor craters, living from a bag of rations, sleeping when he could. And asking questions. Always asking questions.

At a way station, Crater 122, he changed his luck. Joe had worked there tending a solar power plant. From there he'd gone to Crater 139, to Crater 268, 364, to Arzachel, to Crater 631, to Bullialous.

At Bullialous Ransom discovered that

184

he was being followed.

He halted before a detailed map of the area, looking not at the segment of the moon it portrayed but at the reflection in the glass. A shadow drifted behind him, hesitated, moved on to look in the window of a shop — or at the reflection of his quarry in the glass. It was the same man he had seen before. Ransom was certain of it.

He raised a hand and traced a path on the map, letting his finger rest on a crater before lowering it to his side. It had been a random choice, a gesture designed to explain his interest in the map but, as he looked, he frowned in puzzled exasperation.

The path Langdy had taken, the course he had followed swung in a rough circle, which, if continued, would end at Tycho.

★   ★   ★

The communications room at Bullialous was small, the moon-born operator helpful as Ransom explained what he wanted.

185

'I'm sorry, sir.' She seemed genuinely upset. 'Central Agency receive calls from the public through the main desk. Person to person calls are not permitted. They don't want to jam the channels,' she explained.

Ransom didn't answer.

'If you wanted to make an enquiry and it was really urgent you could always go to the local Agency,' she suggested. 'Shall I ring them for you?'

'No.' She was trying to be helpful but it was help he could do without. 'Can you get me the Grand Luna Hotel to Tycho City?' He gave her the number.

'Certainly, sir. Anyone in particular?'

'No. Just the desk.' He put down money. 'This should cover the cost of the call. How long will it take?'

'Not long, Mr. Ransom. If you will wait in the annexe I'll call you.'

The annexe was fitted with chairs, the walls covered with posters, information and regulations. A dispenser offered food and drink. He bought coffee, sipped it, threw the rest into a disposal chute. The speaker called his name.

'My name is Ransom,' he said to the face on the screen. 'I have a room at the hotel. Do you know me?'

'A moment, sir.' The operator looked down as she checked her file. 'I know you, Mr. Ransom.'

'Any messages?'

'Yes, sir. Two.'

'Read them.'

'Yes, sir.' The operator turned, found something, faced the screen again. Her eyes were lowered. 'Message begins — 'Contact me immediately' — message ends. It is signed 'King'.'

'The other?'

'Message begins — 'Have up to the minute information. Party definitely located. Contact me at T1/3/8/112' — message ends. It is signed 'Clerk. R. R'.' The receptionist looked enquiringly at Ransom. 'Shall I connect you?'

'Can you do that on a private line?'

'Certainly, sir.' Ransom waited while the girl punched the number on a second instrument. The screen remained blank. 'I'm afraid there is no answer, sir.'

'All right,' said Ransom. He wished the

record clerk had been more specific but knew why he had not. The man had tasted easy money and wanted more. 'Keep trying to contact that number,' he ordered. 'A fat man should answer. If he does tell him that I'm on my way back now. Ask him to leave a message. If he does, pay him a thousand and put it on my account. Let him know that money is waiting. Get it?'

'Yes, sir, Mr. Ransom.'

Outside the girl operator smiled as she held out his change. He ignored it.

'How soon can I get to Tycho? What's the fastest means of travel? Charter rocket?'

'A moment, sir.' She rang somewhere, spoke, listened, spoke again then cut the connection. 'I'm sorry, sir, but there isn't a charter ship available.' She glanced at the wall-clock. 'The regular commercial flight leaves in thirty minutes.'

'Aside from that?'

'Ground crawler.'

He ran along the passage and into the main area. He made the flight with ten minutes to spare. The rocket was similar to others he had used recently, old, patched, nursed by the crew and kept operating by the exigencies of local requirements.

He relaxed in the worn seat and carefully adjusted the support-padding around his spine. Around him he could hear the usual noises preparatory to take-off, the casual gossip of passengers.

'Did you see the Martian ship?' The voice came from somewhere behind. 'They tell me the Combine is willing to pay ten thousand bounty to any man willing to go. Double for a woman.'

'To Mars?' The second voice was deep and cynical. 'On a one-way ticket? Anyone taking that deal must be crazy.'

'Well, I don't know,' said the first man. 'From what I hear life there can't be all that different. At least you get a clean start. And that ten thousand offer makes a man think.'

'Sure, but money's no good if you can't buy anything with it.' The deep voice was logical. 'Maybe all that ten thousand will buy is a gallon of water or the hire of a suit for a week. Hell, if you want to go to

Mars commit a crime. Do something bad enough and they'll ship you out free. If you're serious you can start by killing my supplier.'

The talk dissolved into laughter. The laughter died as a metallic voice echoed from the speakers.

'Attention, passengers. Take-off in exactly one minute.'

It was then that Ransom recognised a fellow passenger.

He was still being followed.

13

The man was smooth, calm, very polite and very firm.

'I'm sorry, Mr. Delmonte, there is simply nothing we can do. After all, what are you asking? You want us to find someone, you don't know who, to prevent someone else, a Mr. Ransom, from finding him first.' His shrug was one of patronising contempt. 'I know that we perform miracles on the moon but this is a little too much.'

'I don't think so.' With an effort Steve restrained his temper. He had no authority on the moon. In many ways he was worse off than an ordinary tourist; much worse than a resident. They, at least, were protected by the Co-operative Authority. 'I am trying to prevent a crime,' he continued. 'This man Ransom is dangerous. We have reason to suspect that he is guilty of at least one murder.'

'This Mrs. Langdy you told me about?'

'Yes. He was the last man known to have seen her; alive.' Steve tried to think of some way to break the man's calm. 'She died of an alkaloid poison much favoured by assassins.'

'And you are saying that Ransom is an assassin?' The man smiled and shook his head. 'Really, Mr. Delmonte. You Earth Security people are all alike. You start at shadows. What proof have you that Ransom killed the woman?'

'No actual proof,' admitted Steve. 'Just a probability of nine point three per cent. We consider that good enough to subject a suspect to questioning.'

'On Earth!' The man was very sharp. 'But you are on Luna now. Your laws do not apply.'

'I know that.' Steve looked around the office. It had a spartan severity. Two girl clerks were working at an outdated computer. A uniformed man sat at a switchboard. Law enforcement, on the moon, was at a minimum. The essential staff was small.

'Look,' said Steve intently. 'I'm not here to overawe you or to throw my weight around. I haven't any status here and I know it. But equally so I know that you want to protect your own and to prevent crime if you can.'

'So?'

'Ransom landed some time ago. I know that he is looking for someone. Now, assume that you are in his place. How would you go about it?'

'About finding someone whose name I know?'

'Yes.'

The man did not hesitate. 'I would enquire at the Central Agency.'

'Right. Now how would you go about finding out who Ransom wanted to find?'

'I would ask those at the Central Agency who may have dealt with Ransom's enquiry.'

'Right again. Now will you do that please?'

Inwardly Steve sweated waiting for the man to refuse. It would be in character for him to refuse. Steve belonged to Terran Security and so was, in a way, the enemy of Luna. He could only hope that the man's dispassionate regard for law and order would divorce him of any automatic nationalistic tendencies.

'I will look into it,' he said after a moment's thought. 'At least it will do no harm.'

It was all Steve could hope for. Later, while wandering about the maze of Tycho, he halted before a glaring tri-dri display fronting the embassy of the Martian Combine. He became very thoughtful.

Later he went inside.

* * *

Deeper in the city Ransom was waiting. He stood in a corridor in Quadrant one, Decant three, Sector eight. Ahead, round a curve, lay room 112. He had been there before and he was going there again. But the first time he had gone openly — now he moved with caution. He did not want to be seen by any other resident of the sector.

The door was locked. He knocked, waited, knocked again. The latch was flimsy, it yielded to the thrust of his foot.

Inside he closed the door and switched on the light. He stared at what lay on the bed.

The glassy, empty eyes of the fat record clerk stared back at him.

He was quite dead. The ligature around his throat, buried in folds of fat, told how he had finally died. The burns on his bare feet told their own story. He had been tortured, questioned, then killed. Ransom could guess why.

He stood listening but could hear nothing. He crossed the room and put his ear to the door. Again silence. The passage was deserted, the stone sound-proof. A man could scream and not be heard. A man had screamed. Screamed and died.

The room contained nothing of value. He picked up a photograph. It was a triprint in full colour and showed a man and a woman. The man was the clerk, slimmer, younger, handsome in a florid way. The girl was just a girl. Finally he stooped over the body, searched the pockets, forced open the fingers. Nothing. The money he had given the man had vanished. He frowned thoughtfully at the phone.

His hotel number was scrawled on the base-pad. A direct link between him and the dead man.

He removed the top three sheets, tore them into strips, chewed them to a pulp. The faucet was metered. He thrust in coins, drew five ounces of water and swallowed the flat, tasteless liquid. He set down the cup and took a last look round. Caution prickled him with needles of warning. He stepped over to the door and jerked it open.

Two men stood outside.

One of them was the man who had been following him. The other was taller, lighter, more conspicuous. He looked at Ransom, stared past him, stepped into the room.

'Well, well,' he said. 'What's going on here?'

Ransom didn't answer. Instead he backed until the base of his spine hit the edge of the table. It was a flimsy piece of furniture. It slid along behind him until it hit the wall. Resting against it he watched the two men.

'Look at that!' The taller of the two pointed towards the bed. 'Here we are, just a couple of friends paying a visit, and what do we find? Poor old Sam is dead and his killer is just about to leave. Lucky thing we came when we did.'

'Button it up,' said the shorter man. 'Get on the phone and report.'

'Just out of curiosity,' said Ransom. 'How much are you getting for this?'

Neither man answered.

'Whatever it is,' said Ransom. 'I'll double it.' He wasn't reaching them. 'Treble,' he urged. 'Let's say a hundred thousand apiece.'

The tall man hesitated, his hand on the phone.

'For what?'

'For letting me walk out of here. For springing me from this frame.'

'Shut your mouth.' The man who had been following him no longer looked inconspicuous. There was a litheness to his movements, a hardness around the mouth. 'Shut up or I'll do something about it.' He came a little closer.

Ransom kicked him in the groin. He

flung himself forward and to one side, chopping at the tall man's throat. He turned and finished what he had started with the kick. The tall man was retching, clinging to the phone, his free hand clawing at his pocket. Ransom broke his wrist, retained his hold, dragged the injured arm up behind the man's back.

'All right,' he snarled. 'Now talk! Who sent you after me?'

'I don't know. It's the truth, I swear it!' The man writhed, sweating with pain. 'Fred was the boss. I just did as I was told. He phoned me from Bullialous, told me to pick you up at the arrival point, follow you around. I did. I traced you to here, then to the hotel, then back here.'

'Did you help him to do this?'

'No. I was following you. He joined me after you left the hotel. We were to call the police and turn you in.'

'And?'

'I don't know!' The man's voice rose higher as Ransom increased the pressure. 'For God's sake! I don't know anything else!'

'Do you know where Fred got his

orders? The number he phoned? Damn it! Can't you tell me anything I can't guess?'

'You've got the lot, mister. I swear it!' The man whimpered with pain. 'I couldn't tell you more to save my life.'

'No,' said Ransom coldly. 'I don't suppose that you could.'

The edge of his stiffened hand snapped the neck as if it were a stick.

The call was scheduled for midnight. An elevator lifted them to a crystal bubble on the summit of the Palace. A hemisphere of polarised glass, air-conditioned, luxurious. An eyrie for a man who thought of himself as an eagle.

Marcus crossed to a desk and touched a control. The lights faded to a soft, roseate glow. Above and around shone the stars and the silver disc of the moon. Fullen glanced towards it. Up there, at this moment, a man stood before mechanisms which would take his voice and image and hurl them across a quarter of a million miles of emptiness to be resolved in this room. The magic of the ancients, he thought, the science of today.

The screen on the desk lit and Ransom looked at King.

'Hello, Marcus,' he said. 'How are you keeping?'

'Never mind that. Where have you been?'

'Chasing a rainbow. Langdy is the travelling kind. I've been on his trail since I got here.'

'Are you close?'

'Breathing down his neck. I know exactly where he is. Langdy is out at Mare Serenis. His previous travels were either for fun, to gain experience or to raise enough money for equipment. Now he's out prospecting.'

'Mare Serenis?'

'That's right,' said Ransom coldly. 'But you know that already. The men you hired to torture the clerk must have reported what they learned. They knew that he'd given me the same information. That's why they tried to frame me. You wanted me out of the way.'

'David!' Marcus felt a constriction around his heart. 'I don't know what you're talking about.'

'Don't lie to me, Marcus. You've had me followed every step of the way. Now, it seems, I'm no longer needed. Or perhaps you don't want to pay me what you promised.'

'David!' Marcus fought for breath, fighting the blackness edging his vision. Something stung his nostrils and the darkness went away. Irritably he thrust Fullen to one side. 'David, listen to me. I'll give you what I promised. A million in cold cash when you deliver Langdy to the Palace. But I'll do better than that. Get him here alive and well, and we'll forget the past. You can take up the old life again. The King name, David. The King wealth. The King power. We'll share it, David. All of it.'

'Begging, Marcus?'

'Yes, David. I want Langdy. Get him and you can have what you ask.'

'You couldn't begin to pay what I want Marcus,' Ransom's smile was cold, vicious. 'But I'll find Langdy. And when I do, I'll kill him!'

The screen wavered, died, grew dark as the connection was broken.

'Steady!' Fullen reached for Marcus a hypogun in his hand. Air hissed as it blasted its charge directly through the skin and into the blood. Marcus snarled and sent it spinning to the floor.

'Damn you, Fullen! I don't need your dope. You heard what he said?'

'He didn't mean it.'

'Didn't he?' Marcus paused, calming as the drug took effect. 'Maybe not,' he said softly. 'But, in any case, he won't get the chance.'

Fullen looked at the moon as he stooped to pick up the hypogun. Marcus followed his glance.

'Strange, isn't it, Fullen? Up there is a man who has everything I want and yet he's living like a pig. Prospecting. Transient worker. Living in filth with nothing to call his own. Why should such a man be given such a gift?'

Fullen didn't answer.

'Why isn't he rich?' continued Marcus. 'Why isn't he one of the rulers of this planet? The only ruler. Why, Fullen? Why?'

'You are mortal,' said the doctor evenly.

'And yet you are the target for assassins. Doesn't that answer your question?'

'A man can protect himself against assassination.'

'Can he protect himself against the envious hatred of the world?'

'There are ways,' said Marcus. 'But poor? Why is he poor?'

'Maybe he's jaded,' said Fullen. 'Maybe he's learned what we never seem to learn. A man can only do so much. If he owns a hundred palaces each with a thousand rooms he can only be in one at a time. Perhaps he is tired, bored with the endless routine of existence.'

'Then he is a fool!' Marcus felt the tension around his heart, the sudden pain. It was a strong heart, a young heart, it should not feel pain. If he ignored it, it would go away.

He had thought like that as a child.

He sat and felt the old, familiar depression. The horrible introversion born of his dread and insecurity. The fear born of his terror of death.

And yet he did not think of dying. Instead he thought of all the things he had done — and could never do again.

The knowledge that this might be the last time he would sit in this room. The last time he would look at the stars and moon. That he had eaten his last meal. Death was like that. Death was regret at wasted opportunity. Its real horror rested in the uncompromising finality of its total erasure.

To die. To cease to be.

'No!' he screamed. 'No! No!'

He sprang to his feet and glared at the moon.

'It's there! The secret! Langdy has it and, when I have him, I'll find it if I have to take him apart cell by cell! I won't die! I —'

Then the pain in his heart grew to encompass the world.

14

Seen from Earth the Mare Serenis is relatively flat, a rolling plain of featureless nothingness, a dark patch on the face of the moon. Seen at first hand it is nothing like that. It is a desert of dust-filled craters, of mighty dunes and the nubs of mountains. It is stark, barren, treacherous with hidden dangers, an airless hell. Yet it holds wealth and so there are men.

Ransom wasn't looking for wealth. He wasn't interested in deposits of meteoric iron, air and water bearing rock or the freak-gems created by the impact of stones from space against the native rock. He was looking for a man.

He halted, leaning against a wall of stone, feeling sweat over his face, irritating with a thousand tiny stings. His back itched, he had a rash on the insides of both legs, his armpits felt raw. Locked in his suit he felt helpless. It was a feeling he didn't enjoy.

'Something wrong?'

The voice came from the speaker behind his ear. Ahead of him the guide, brilliant in his orange suit, stood patiently waiting.

'There's nothing wrong.' Ransom blinked sweat from his eyes. 'I'm just looking around.'

'Look all you want,' said Clinton. 'But if you want to enjoy the view you'd better get in the shade. There's no sense in getting hotter than you have to.'

'Never mind,' said Ransom. 'Let's get moving.'

They had been moving for days. Walking, scrambling over rocky mounds, circumnavigating patches of dust finer than talc, more deadly than quicksand, edging along crevasses. Their progress had seen slow.

Too slow. There had been too many delays at the beginning. It had taken him too long to find a willing guide. Ransom was filled with a sense of urgency, the knowledge that time was running out. King would not have been idle. He had to find Langdy first.

He stumbled, swayed as a hand gripped his harness, teetered on the edge of a shallow concavity. He could hear the harsh sound of Clinton's breath as the guide pulled him back.

'Do that again,' he snapped, 'and I'll let you go. Damn it, man, how often must I tell you to keep both eyes open and your mind on the job?'

Ransom bit back his instinctive reply.

'That's a sucker,' said Clinton. 'Look.' He picked up a stone and tossed it gently over the edge. It vanished as if falling into water. 'That could have been you. How deep they are no one knows. The only thing we can be sure about is that once in you don't get out.' He paused. 'I lost a good partner that way.'

'I'm sorry,' said Ransom. 'About your partner, I mean.'

'Well, it happens. It taught me never to take anything for granted. Never to trust anything in the Serenis. The fact that I got back alone shows how well I learned.'

They walked for another mile in silence then: 'How's your temperature?'

Ransom looked at the dials set above his faceplate.

'High. Well into the red.'

'Can you make it to that crest?' The orange figure lifted an arm and pointed. 'It's about another mile. Make it and we'll camp.

Camping was a matter of unfolding the tent, climbing inside, sealing the vent and inflating it with air from their suit-tanks. The air carried most of the internal heat with it as it expanded. Clinton checked the seals, examined the fabric, released more air. Satisfied he opened his faceplate. Together they helped each other from the suits.

Food was something out of a can. Drink was water, tepid, brackish, flavoured with lemon. Modesty was, by necessity, totally absent.

They didn't talk, Ransom was too tired for that. Gingerly he stretched himself full-length, watching Clinton as he checked the air-reviver, the pressure gauge, the mechanism that controlled the humidity. The man was paper-white aside from his face, which was tanned from barely shielded ultra violet. But there was nothing soft about the whiteness. Muscles rippled in trained economy as he went through the routine check. He was very thorough. Their lives hung on his caution.

Finally, satisfied, he settled down to sleep.

'Goodnight,' he said.

'Goodnight,' said Ransom.

★　★　★

It wasn't night. It was just a pause in activity, a time to eat and rest and shed the chafing prison of the suits.

Ransom was too tired to fall immediately asleep. He lay and stared at the low apex of the tent, the fabric taut beneath the eight pounds pressure. The air-reviver made a thin, whirring sound as the fans sucked the air through the unit. The pressure gauge remained steady, the alarm that would sound if it fell silent. The humidifier sighed as it adjusted the moisture content of the atmosphere. Clinton breathed with a monotonous regularity that told he was asleep.

Ransom considered whether to kill him now.

He decided against it. In a few hours they would have to rise, dress, pump back the air into the cans, fold the tent and be on their way. Alone Clinton could do it. Random doubted if he could manage as well. In any case there was no immediate need. Later would do as well.

Later, when they had found Langdy.

He fell asleep dreaming of a face. It had no features but, somehow, he knew that it was terribly important. It spelt wealth, security, prestige. It was safety, the key to the prison door, money in the bank. It was a weapon. It was revenge. Without it he was nothing.

Nothing!

He stretched out his hands and was running but, as fast as he ran, the face receded. And, as it dwindled, it changed. It grew a nose, eyes, a mane of hair, a cynical, sneering expression.

Marcus!

Marcus Edward King!

He woke, drenched in sweat, trembling.

Clinton's hand was on his shoulder, his face very close.

'You all right?'

'Yes.' Ransom sat upright. His muscles had grown stiff, the chafes burned with fire.

'You sure?' The guide was doubtful. 'You were screaming.'

'I had a dream.' Ransom felt giddy. He lowered his head until the feeling passed. 'Just a dream.'

'Dreams can be bad,' said Clinton. 'I dreamed a lot after my partner died. You know, the one I told you about. He kept screaming for me to help him out of the dust. I couldn't help him. He should have known that. But he kept pleading, praying, begging. I couldn't turn off my radio. It seemed to last for hours.'

'Nice,' said Ransom shortly. He winced as he moved. 'How about getting on our way?'

'Sure,' said Clinton. 'Just as you say.'

They decamped and left the crest. They walked down a slope that ended in a ledge, which fell away in a shattered mass of detritus. They crossed, climbed a ridge, followed a crevasse too wide to jump, too deep to climb. The crevasse ended and they were climbing again. Clinton, in the lead, halted beside a mass of fused and shattered stone.

'Something wrong?' Ransom joined him, watched as he searched the ground. 'Let's get going.'

'Hold it a minute.' Clinton stooped, clawed at the stone, lifted something in his gloved hand. Tiny jewels winked fire. 'Freak-gems. Small but there could be more.'

'Forget them.'

'They're worth maybe a hundred apiece back at the depot,' protested the guide. 'Big ones up to ten times as much. It won't take long to search the area.'

'To hell with the stuff,' snarled Ransom. 'I pay you to act as guide, not to look for loot. Come on!'

Clinton obeyed.

Two hours later Ransom pushed him off a ledge.

$\star$ $\star$ $\star$

Clinton vanished at once. One second he was standing, bright orange against the sky, the next he had gone, sinking into the dust like a pebble in liquid mud. Even the radio remained silent. Ransom was glad of that.

He stood, breathing deeply, forgetting the pain of his raw flesh as he looked ahead. In the far distance a spot of colour shone against the grey monotony of the Serenis. Only one thing could have made that splotch of brilliance. A tent. An encampment. Langdy!

'Hello!' called Ransom into his radio. 'Hello, can anyone hear me?'

No answer.

Ransom wasn't disappointed. The man could be asleep, shielded by metallic rock, too cautious to reply, anything But he was there, the splotch of colour proved that.

An hour later it was nearer but still the radio remained silent. Doggedly Ransom forged ahead. Slipping, walking in cautious slowness, concentrating on every inch of the way. Once he slipped and rolled towards a crevasse. Once he stumbled and almost fell into a patch of silken-smooth dust. Three times he made wide detours around real or fancied dangers.

Alone the going was tough but, on the way back, he wouldn't be alone. Langdy would be with him. He would guide them both back to safety. A lamb leading himself to the slaughter. Ransom found the thought amusing. It was the only thing to smile at. He was almost totally exhausted when he reached the tent.

It was larger than the one Clinton had carried. It had a small airlock protruding from one side. The outer vestibule was empty, proof that the occupier was absent, but he didn't think of that as he passed through the lock into the tent. Inside he opened his faceplate and gulped at the stagnant air.

There was water in a can. He helped himself. There was a little food, tasteless pulp in emergency containers. There was a powerful radio. He switched it on.

Music spilled from the speaker, relayed from orbiting satellites, beamed from the major Luna cities. The music faded, a gong echoed, a man's voice read a weather report.

' . . . sunspot activity promises a dangerously high rate of radiation. All ground-operators on sunside are warned to make preparations to protect themselves. New bulletins will be broadcast as the flare approaches.' A click and the voice was speaking again, this time in a foreign language. Irritably Ransom switched off the set.

Where the hell was Langdy?

Restlessly he searched the interior of the tent, looking at everything which might carry a name, which might hold papers, which would make a supposition into a certainty. Clinton had guided him here. Clinton had known the object of his search. He would not have guided him wrong.

Or would he?

Whatever he had been the guide had proved himself a liar No true prospector would have passed up the chance to mine a strike of gems. His obedience in obeying the order to move had crystallised Ransom's suspicions. Clinton could have been planted. But Langdy?

Ransom sat down and forced his brain

to do its job. He had evidence, the tent, the contents of the tent He looked at them and this time weighed and considered what he saw.

A little food. A little water. Stagnant air. Articles which were nameless, things a man might collect and then discard if he was on the move.

And Langdy had been out when he arrived.

How long had he been gone?

Ransom snarled as he realised the truth. An experienced man would have known at once but he was vague as to the customs of the Serenis. Now it was obvious.

The tent was too big to be carried. It was a permanent installation, hired by those who wanted to use it as a base-camp, left as he had found it when no longer required. He had misread the signs and had wasted time.

Time!

Ransom surged to his feet. Even now Langdy could be on his way to the depot and, from there, where? He had to find him before he got too far. Slamming shut his faceplate he crawled into the airlock, sealed the inner door, sweated as he pumped air back into the cans. The effort was too much. Irritably he ripped open the outer seal and felt himself blasted into the vacuum.

Outside he searched for footprints, found too many, thinned his lips at the puzzle they represented. One set wended to the north, the direction from which Clinton had guided him, and Ransom followed them from want of a better guide.

An hour later he lost the trail on the naked stone of a worn mountain.

Thirty minutes after that the radio in his helmet crackled to strident life.

'Attention! Warning to all sunside personnel. The solar flare is reaching prominence and max radiation will reach us in approximately thirty minutes. Attention! All sunside . . . '

Ransom ignored the voice. He stood swaying, soaked with perspiration, the chafed places on his body burning with pain. He gritted his teeth and forged ahead. He had no choice but to continue.

The tent had been carried by Clinton and had vanished with him. Without it he had no option but to stay in the confines of his suit.

The radio repeated its warning.

'Attention! All sunside personnel. Max radiation in fifteen minutes!'

'Go to hell!' snarled Ransom. He licked parched lips and tongued the nipple from his canteen into his mouth. The water was too warm to be refreshing. He spat out the nipple and looked at the dials monitoring his little world. The water was low. The liquid food was low. The temperature was high. The external radiation was the same and climbing higher.

The forerunner of the radiation from the solar flare.

To remain in the open was to die.

The tent would have helped but he had lost the tent.

All he could do was to find a cave and crawl into it and hope that it would be protection enough. But there were no caves. The nearest hills were miles away. He looked back. There was no help to his rear. There was no help anywhere.

'Attention!' snapped the radio. 'Max radiation in five minutes. If you're not under cover now you should be. Max radiation in five minutes!'

A humped ledge of rock stood to the right. It might just be possible to find an overhang and squeeze under it. It wouldn't be complete protection but some exposure he could tolerate. More could be treated if he could get to a hospital in time. But first he had to reach the shelter.

Ransom began to run towards it. A dust-filled crater lay between him and the ledge. He veered to the right, trod on a loose piece of stone, lost his balance — and fell into the dust.

He screamed once with the horror of it. He knew that he was going to die.

15

The vestibule of the Palace had been fashioned as a replica of the Sistine Chapel complete with facsimiles of the famous paintings. Dale Markham studied them with interest, turning as Steve joined him. The agent looked harder, thinner. He carried a brief case.

'Ready?'

'Ready and waiting,' said the chief. He hesitated. 'Are you sure that you want me with you?'

'You were in at the beginning,' said Steve. He kept his voice low as did all visitors to the vestibule. 'You might as well be in at the end. King is waiting for us in the hospital. I suppose that he's in bed.'

King wasn't in bed. He sat in a padded chair, wearing a robe of watered silk, a flask of oxygen at his side. His face was drawn, the skin grey, the eye febrile. Fullen stood beside him. The doctor was very calm.

'Mr. King has had a heart attack,' he said. 'I must ask you not to excite him unduly.'

'Shut up, Fullen.' Marcus didn't look at the doctor. 'This is important.'

'Very important,' said Steve. He rested the briefcase on the floor beside his chair. 'I know who tried to kill you, Mr. King — and why.'

Marcus closed his eyes. He seemed very old and very frail and very afraid. He looked at Steve as he continued.

'In every crime there are three components: means, method and motive. We know the means, a plane was crashed into the room in which you slept. The attempt to kill you failed because of sheer, blind luck. The method was not so obvious. Who arranged it? Who planned it? How was it carried out? Murder is a personal crime, Mr. King. Men are killed through hate, fear or greed or because they are dangerous to some other person or persons. We suspected the Cartel but, from what we could discover, they had no motive. That reduced the field to a personal level.'

'And that, of course, answered all your questions?' Marcus was sneering. Steve refused to become annoyed.

'Yes, Mr. King,' he said calmly. 'It did.'

He lifted his brief case, opened it, took out a compact portable recorder. He rested it on his lap.

'As I said murder is a personal crime. We had certain persons who were automatically suspect. Murray, the pilot of the plane. His wife Stella. Her friend Ransom. Klien the owner of the plane. Let us take Ransom. David C. Ransom. The man who once had reason to believe that he was to be your adoptive heir.'

'I never — ' began Marcus, then paused. 'It was an assumption he had no right to make,' he finished. Steve shrugged.

'When you turn a man from a prince into a pauper you supply him with a pretty strong reason to wish you dead. Ransom knew Murray's wife. It is inconceivable that he did not know Murray. Murray was poor, his wife liked excitement and luxury, Ransom had money to provide both. When he suggested they go on holiday together she jumped at the offer. They were together during the time of the attempt on your life.'

'I know that,' snapped Marcus irritably. 'I checked. His alibi was foolproof.'

'Then why didn't you accept it?'

'I don't understand.'

'Yes you do, Mr. King. You believed that Ransom had engineered that attempt on your life. You may have thought that he'd sold out to the Cartel. Whatever the reason you suspected him.'

'Ridiculous! Why, I even gave him a job. Isn't that proof that I thought him innocent?'

'No, the reverse, as he knew all along.' Steve lifted the lid of the recorder, pressed a button. 'Listen to this, Mr. King.'

The voice was thin, wavering but it held an unmistakable horror. When it had ended sweat shone on Marcus's forehead.

'A man named Clinton took this recording,' said Steve. 'He is connected with Luna Security. I managed to obtain their co-operation. He met Ransom and guided him on a long and time-wasting route to his objective. In return Ransom tried to kill him. Only his ignorance and Clinton's skill thwarted his intention. Clinton was pushed into some harmless dust. He lay still until it was safe to crawl out and followed Ransom when he headed back to the depot. They were caught in a storm. Clinton knew how to look after himself. Ransom didn't. He fell into the dust and died there.' He gestured towards the recorder. 'As you heard he didn't die at once. He fought to the last.'

'Yes,' said Marcus dully. 'He would.'

'He hated you,' said Steve flatly. 'He'd hated you since you kicked him out. He was going to find Langdy and kill him. That was the one sure way he could obtain the greatest revenge. To kill something you wanted so desperately.'

'I didn't trust him,' admitted King.

'That's why you tried to frame him for murder. He knew that you were responsible. He even thought he knew why the clerk had been tortured but he was wrong about that. The man was tortured because the penalty for murder with aggravation is the worst there is on the moon. You wanted him to suffer that. The fact that his death was even worse must be a consolation to you.'

Steve stooped, put the recorder in the brief case, closed the snap.

'A nice revenge, Mr. King. But entirely unwarranted. Ransom was not responsible for the attempt on your life.'

Fullen stepped forward as Marcus clutched at his chest. His face whitened as King knocked aside his hand.

'Get away from me!' Marcus looked at Steve. 'It isn't true. David — '

'Had nothing to do with that crash,' interrupted Steve. His only connection was that he knew Murray's wife, perhaps Murray himself, and a woman named Linda Sheldon.' He looked at Marcus. 'Do you know her?'

Marcus shook his head.

'She is a relative of Patricia McKee. She was propositioned to make illegal krowns. She needed money and so agreed. But she was curious as to the identity of her client. She recorded his voice. It was disguised but there are unmistakable points of similarity. The man was Ransom.

'But doesn't that prove his connection?' It was the first time Fullen had shown interest. 'Why else should he want to deal in adapted krowns?'

'For money.' Steve was curt, he did not want to talk about Linda's part in the affair. 'All of Ransom's actions can be explained by his hate and greed. All of them. But he had no direct knowledge or connection with the attempt on your life, Mr. King.'

'You know who has?'

'Yes.' Steve paused, very conscious of Fullen's eyes. 'We have to go back to Ransom,' he said. 'He worked on the fringe. He knew Murray, a drifter with a beautiful and bored wife, eager and willing to earn money how he could. Murray knew Klien who owns a circus and racing planes. Klien knew Mark Sheldon, a rocket-race pilot who had suffered terrible injuries in a crash. Mark Sheldon whose sister is an accomplished electronician with the skill and knowledge to adapt krowns.

'Ransom was the go-between. Mark was as good as dead — Murray had no real reason for staying alive. It doesn't take genius to see the obvious. Mark, by means of a master/slave control could govern Murray's body. Murray, for the sake of money, was to co-operate. Klien, for the same reason, was a willing partner. Between them they had a nice racket.

'Murray sat in the cockpit while Mark flew the plane. They raced and who would bet on an unknown like Murray to win? Only Murray wasn't the pilot, Mark was, and he was one of the best rocket-race pilots known. Klien shared in the take and kept his mouth shut. That is the reason he wasn't worried when the plane left the field. As far as he knew Murray, under Mark's control, had taken it up for a practice flight. When the truth came out be denied knowing Murray at all. He lied.

'Mark's sister denied making him a master/slave control. She also lied. She probably imagined that the krowns were to be used on a non-human proxy like a monkey or a dog. That is the full extent of her complicity.'

'But — ' commenced Markham. Steve looked at him and he coughed and fell silent.

'The man who drove the plane into this building in an attempt to kill Mr. King was Mark Sheldon. His motive was one of pure hate. He considered that his maternal aunt, Patricia McKee, had been robbed of her rightful share in the profits of the McKee effect.'

'That is a lie!' Marcus stirred in his chair.

'Perhaps.' Steve had his own ideas. 'But to a man, hopelessly crippled, almost destitute, the niceties of legal abstractions are a little hard to follow. His aunt had discovered the basis for the krowns. She had died in poverty while the man who commercialised her discovery became even more wealthy. He would consider it a good motive for murder.'

'Is that all?' Fullen had been standing very quietly behind the chair. Steve met his eyes.

'That is all. The main participants are dead. Klien denies all knowledge of the set-up and cannot, legally, be touched.'

'And the sister?' Fullen hesitated. 'Miss Sheldon?'

'She adapted the krowns for research purposes only,' said Steve blandly. 'The other matter has been investigated and no official action is contemplated.'

'And that is all?'

'That is all.'

'I see.' Fullen looked down at his hands. Steve knew what he was thinking. Three men had died during the attempt to kill King. They had yet to be avenged.

'The case is closed,' he said quickly. He picked up the briefcase and rose. Marcus stirred where he sat.

'Wait!' His voice was thin, desperate. 'What about Langdy?'

'Yes,' said Steve. 'Joe Langdy, the man you wanted desperately to find. So desperately that you sent Ransom after him knowing that, driven by hate as he was, he would be far more efficient than a man merely driven greed. Langdy is on his way to Mars. I learned that when I enquired at their embassy in Tycho. The Luna authorities delayed Ransom long enough for him to make ship.'

★ ★ ★

Fullen showed them out. He was very quiet, very thoughtful. He hesitated before handing them over to the guard waiting beyond earshot down the corridor.

'Mr. King has had a terrible shock,' he said as if speaking to himself. 'He collapsed and almost died. He forgets that, though you can graft a young man's heart into an old body, the body is still old. The unknown factor that causes age infects the younger organ. I am speaking broadly, you understand.'

Steve nodded.

'And there are psychosomatic difficulties. His overwhelming terror of death is developing into a deep psychosis which — ' He broke off as if about to divulge confidential information. But Steve understood what he left unsaid.

Marcus Edward King was a man with

nothing to look forward to but insanity and death.

'Goodbye, doctor.' Steve held out his hand. 'Goodbye — and thank you.'

He was silent as they walked down the corridor. Silent as the elevator lined them to ground level. Silent as they walked through the replica of the Sistine Chapel and towards the doors of the Palace. Markham halted beside a tinkling fountain.

'You lied,' he said. 'Why?'

'Sufficient unto the day is the evil thereof,' said Steve as he had once before. 'Are you answered?'

'No.'

'Then let the dead bury the dead.'

'Including those patrol men who died?'

'Even those.' Steve turned and looked at the chief. 'So I covered up, I admit it, but it was a last-minute decision. I was going to clean the whole thing up, throw you a victim, prove how clever I was. Well, I changed my mind. There will be no victim.'

'So Fullen gets away with it,' said Markham.

'You guessed?'

'I saw his face. He knew that you suspected him. It's obvious when you stop to think about it. He was the only man who could have directed the plane to its target. The only man, aside from the guard, who knew where Marcus was to be found that night. And the guard died saving King's life.'

'He didn't think of that,' said Steve. 'King was too convinced that Ransom was getting his revenge to realise that, if the attack was to succeed, the pilot would have to know where to aim the plane. Fullen knew. After he left he had only to make one phone call.'

'And two patrol men died because of it,' reminded the chief. 'Not counting the guard.'

'Yes.'

'And you're letting him get away with it?'

'I am.'

Markham sighed and shook his head. He looked annoyed and a little baffled.

'I've been in the police long enough to learn that justice isn't the abstract thing it's supposed to be,' he said. 'But I'm curious. Just how is it done?'

'Fullen is connected with Doctor Linguard,' said Steve. 'I think that one of the reasons he agreed to work for King was because he needed the money to support the clinic. He would have known about Mark and the master/slave control. To them both it would have been harmless enough. Relief for a cripple and, at the same time, data for their research. But, at the same time, it gave them a weapon in case of need.'

'The krown,' said Markham. 'You didn't mention the blow-box. Did Linguard fix it?'

'Probably, but we could never prove it. In any case his subconscious wouldn't let him commit deliberate murder. The thing didn't work.'

'More whitewash,' said Markham with disgust. 'Maybe you should give them a medal.'

'Linda said that,' mused Steve. 'As it happens she was perfectly correct. The motive tells us that. Fullen knew of King's search for immortality. He knew him too well to have any illusions as to what would happen if he managed to achieve longevity. You heard him talk about his psychotic condition. We know of his scheme to turn the world into a captive audience. A scheme, incidentally, which would work.'

'But not now?'

'Not unless we're bigger fools than I imagine.' Steve paused, wondering, then shrugged. 'To get back to Fullen. When he left King that night he was upset. He probably called Linguard almost at once. Mark was dying and time was running out. If King had to be stopped they could afford no delay. So Linguard told Mark just where King was to be found. He did the rest.'

'And failed.'

'He didn't manage to kill King but he didn't fail. The crash brought us on the scene. It started a chain of events ending in now. Without it who knows what might have happened? Cheap krowns everywhere. Sub-aural commands. King maybe finding what he was looking for and firm in the saddle as he rode out a financial war. No, Mark did not fail.'

'And now what?' said Markham. Steve smiled.

'Fullen stays with King. King is dying. If, in his insanity, he tries to do what should not be done — well, we have Fullen at his side.'

'Neat,' said Markham. He looked as if he tasted something bad. 'Sly, cunning and effective. Now I know why Security is so successful. You relinquish a killer to gain a potential assassin. Nice.'

'Essential. How else can we combat the money-power of the tycoons?'

'I don't know,' admitted Markham. 'But there must be a better way.' He shook his head in a symbolical shedding of responsibility. 'And what about Langdy? Did he really go to Mars?'

'That was true enough.'

'And is he really — ?'

'Immortal?' Steve shrugged. 'I don't know. I didn't ask. He could be a freak, someone who just keeps on living while other men die. I simply don't know. I don't think I want to know. I don't want to be another King.'

'No,' said Markham. 'One is enough.'

Together they walked from the fountain, past the old, cold statuary, towards the doors and the sun, the living world outside.

THE END

We do hope that you have enjoyed reading this large print book.

Did you know that all of our titles are available for purchase?

We publish a wide range of high quality large print books including:

Romances, Mysteries, Classics
General Fiction
Non Fiction and Westerns

Special interest titles available in large print are:

The Little Oxford Dictionary
Music Book, Song Book
Hymn Book, Service Book

Also available from us courtesy of Oxford University Press:

Young Readers' Dictionary
(large print edition)
Young Readers' Thesaurus
(large print edition)

For further information or a free brochure, please contact us at:
Ulverscroft Large Print Books Ltd.,
The Green, Bradgate Road, Anstey,
Leicester, LE7 7FU, England.
Tel: (00 44) **0116 236 4325**
Fax: (00 44) **0116 234 0205**

ODD WOMAN OUT

George Douglas

Chief Inspector Bill Hallam and sergeant 'Jack' Spratt of the Deniston C.I.D. are investigating the death of Madge Adkin. The dead woman had peculiar habits and claimed to be a bird-watcher, but knew nothing about birds. The trail they follow leads them to an escaped prisoner, an unorthodox 'healer' and a bunch of anonymous letters . . . The killer seems to have covered his tracks, but a blackmail attempt, quite unconnected with the murder, brings the detectives the proof they need.

CALLERS FOR DR. MORELLE

Ernest Dudley

In his Harley Street house, Dr. Morelle listens to Thelma Grayson describe how, the previous night, she had shot Ray Mercury. Thelma explains that Mercury had been responsible for her sister's suicide. The morning newspapers reported that Mercury had shot himself. Now, Thelma asks if she should give herself up to the police, or let them believe he shot himself? Morelle's search for the answer finds him and Miss Frayle adventuring into Soho's dark underworld, before finally trapping the murderer.

ROBBERY WITHOUT VIOLENCE

John Russell Fearn

When fifty million pounds worth of gold vanishes overnight from an impregnable bank vault, Chief Inspector Hargraves of Scotland Yard finds himself completely baffled. And when the owner of the bank dies in mysterious circumstances, Hargraves is again spurred to seek outside help from scientist Sawley Garson, a specialist in solving 'impossible' crimes. But can even he explain the inexplicable?

THE GIRL HUNTERS

Sydney J. Bounds

Doll Winters was a naïve teenager, who fantasised about being a film character. But when Gerald Dodd committed a brutal killing, she found herself starring in a real-life murder drama — as the star witness! And when Dodd tries to silence her, Doll turns for help to the famous private detective Simon Brand. Then a further terrifying attempt on her life forces her to go on the run. But can Brand find her before the killer can?